Copyright

All rights reserved, i[t is illegal to]
reproduce this book,
in any form. No part of this text may be reproduced,
transmitted, downloaded, decompiled, reverse
engineered, or stored in or introduced to any
information storage and retrieval system, in any form
or by any means, whether electronic or mechanical
without the express written permission of the author.
The scanning, uploading, and distribution of this book
via the internet or via any other means without the
permission of the author is illegal and punishable by
law. Please purchase only authorised electronic
editions and do not participate in, or encourage,
electronic piracy of these copyrighted materials.

## Acknowledgements

The author would like to thank David Walker, Lauren Greenway and Angela Newman for their help, support and input into the creation of NO ANGEL.


Cover Design – Shiny Demon Design

Cover eyes – Chelsea Amanda Blake

# About the Author

Nigel Shinner is a Pembrokeshire born and raised author with a deep interest in the hidden parts of human behaviour and a vivid imagination. Personally, Nigel is a larger than life character, with a sharp wit and a wicked sense of humour, although his taste in fiction, whether written or on screen, is often from the darker side of the human condition, with psychological thrillers being a firm favourite.

Throughout his working career, Nigel has always loved meeting and interacting with new people, and his various jobs have allowed him to travel to the four corners of the United Kingdom. And although he has been to many wild and wonderful places in England, Northern Ireland and Scotland, nowhere he has been will replace his beloved Wales, or more specifically, the county of Pembrokeshire.

The words may come easy now but that was not always the case. Whilst in school, Nigel was not a fan of academia, with English being his least favourite subject thus leading him to do very badly in his final examinations. Although, he did develop a passion for reading after his school life had ended, especially the reading of true crime and horror fiction. This sparked the idea that he himself could also write such stories.

After a half-hearted attempted at a creative writing course and several efforts to write a worthy story over a fifteen year period, Nigel eventually found his focus and succeeded in completing his first book FROM WITHIN, a detective story that looks back into a cold war project of the CIA that erupts in the present day. This was released via Amazon in the spring of 2015.

The release of FROM WITHIN was swiftly followed up by THE LEGACY, a stand-alone crime thriller, significantly darker and more violent story than FROM WITHIN, it is not for the feint hearted. Nigel's desire in this novel was to expand and stretch his writing muscles to see how much his readers would embrace and challenge his own writing abilities. THE LEGACY was written over the middle months of 2015 whilst fully marketing the debut FROM WITHIN at the same time.

Both novels have received dozens of five star reviews from across the globe and there is a hungry market awaiting the next Nigel Shinner release.

And that wait is now over.

As always, for my children.

mindsweeper

/mynd:swi-per/

*Noun*

1) CIA funded, Cold War project that researched the possible uses of psychic phenomena for military purposes.

2) A person considered to possess inexplicable psychic powers, who can execute invasive mind process, to read memories and effect mind control through simple thought.

# NO ANGEL

## By

## NIGEL SHINNER

# Chapter One

The deep blackness of the night swallowed any light like a black hole. The freezing cold winter air had all but sucked the oxygen from his lungs. His mind had been taken, lost to someone that had such a power that a mind could easily be taken. The only emotion that still resided at the forefront of his consciousness was fear. Fear of the unknown. Fear of what was to come. Fear of the hidden enemy that dwelled within his mind, controlling every step, every movement, every act that forced him towards his fate.

James Shriver was most comfortable when sitting behind his affluent wooden desk, dressed in Italian suits and choosing exotic destinations to jet off to for the weekend. He was not accustomed to stumbling across grassland on a moonless night. Expensive, bespoke leather shoes, wholly unsuitable for floundering through fields in the dead of night, were plastered in mud. The branches of nearby trees snagged his suit jacket, ripping it from his back, leaving only the thin material of a shirt to protect his soft, overfed, middle aged body against the stifling, murky night.

He collided with a dividing hedgerow. The darkness made it impossible to see, although his eyes could see nothing, as he no longer controlled his senses. His senses were in the charge of a Mindsweeper.

The Mindsweeper, a highly skilled and gifted psychic, manipulated the synapsis and pushed Shriver's body through the dense foliage barrier. Not with hands, but with conscious thought, driving his limbs through the tearing undergrowth, forcing a way through to reach the path on the other side.

If Shriver's senses had been able to feedback to his mind, then the sight and sound of rapidly moving vehicles would have overpowered him. Deafening engine roar and glaring headlights punched a hole in the midnight gloom. Even at this time of night the freeway traffic was still heavy.

His body was compelled to walk to the centre of the overpass. A dense cloud of exhaust fumes created a minute pocket of warm air, which offered no comfort against the chill. He stopped directly above the fast moving outer lane. The moment was being calculated.

The Mindsweeper could see the cars flowing toward the overpass, but not with their own eyes, with Shriver's. They used his arms and his legs to mount the low railing. Patience was required. The timing had to be perfect but the mental intrusion could not be maintained for much longer. The cerebral grip would soon be lost if too many external factors seeped through. The fear and the chill were undermining the link. Coldness started to penetrate the veil of control imposed upon him. The final sensation that would accompany Shriver's mind into the oblivion of death was that of icy terror.

Time was of the essence.

But then, a row of three cars, close together and moving fast.

Now is the time. The push off from the railings was an effort. The body moved. The body fell. Perfect.

James Shriver's body hit the tarmac hard with a sickening crunch, a second before the first car ploughed over his fleshy body. Enough time for his mind to be released and regain full sensory control; for him to be fully aware and experience his own death.

A second car also hit the now lifeless form, hooking a limb into the suspension and dragging the corpse until the brakes did their job.

The road closed that night and did not reopen until the dawn.

Part one of the task was complete.

In the darkened room, her eyes flickered open; eyes as black as a pitch black night to match her long, curled, flowing hair. A fine sweat had formed on her brow, her breathing laboured. It had been close. The link had nearly been lost. Next time she might need to be closer to the target or not take the risk of external factors compromising her will.

She opened the door to the garden, letting the brilliant morning sunlight flood the rented house. The warmth comforting her as the chill of the night, five thousand miles away, left her senses.

The distance was keeping her safe, for now, but it would not protect her for long, for there were others like her, hunting her down. She was special - she was powerful. She had successfully evaded capture so far. But it would not last. She knew it and would need help. Help from another - another like her.

# Chapter Two

The worst part of the day; the morning commute. Bristol was always a nightmare to negotiate between 7am. and 7pm.Unfortunately, for Raymond Dean, it was between these hours he liked to work. It was swings and roundabouts, the better the drive across the city, the more unsociable the hour. Today he was stuck behind a car transporter. A vehicle that needed more room than the road often allowed. Overtaking was risky, especially as there was always some joker trying to force their way through the traffic like it was a god given rite.

Ray decided that he would just settle for being a tad late. His partner in crime, or more accurately, partner in investigation, Mike 'Barney' Barnett, would always be in before Ray to deal with any emergency situation. Unless, that is, Barney was on a stake out, but today there was nothing planned so normal service would continue.

Ray and Barney had built a very successful private investigation business, mostly on the back of commercial investigation and wayward spouses. If they were honest, every day was different. Every case was different. Some were long winded and boring, with weeks of surveillance leading to nothing of particular interest to the investigation team, but absolutely vital to the client with results that were gratifying but somewhat predictable.

Other cases were exciting, fast paced, intriguing; as though from the pages of a great novel. Commercial espionage was a particular interest to Barney. He liked to sniff out the culprits using good old fashioned gut feeling, detective work and when all else failed, Barney would throw in a large degree of technology in the form of micro cameras, bugs and spyware. Either way, the agency always excelled and figured out the truth.

Ray, on the other hand, preferred all the family orientated cases such as missing persons, reuniting estranged families with loved ones or the darker, yet ultimately fascinating, domestic investigations. Over the years, Ray had built up a blue print for suspicious husbands or wives to follow. It was not a hundred percent reliable but pretty close and acted as a guide to see whether there had been some infidelity within the relationship. If a middle aged man starts to take care of his appearance after years of not caring at all, then it's a first warning sign to a jaded wife that there could be trouble ahead. Equally, if a wife develops a new social circle, spends more and more time in the company of others, then it's an indication of a change in attitude. Neither of these is a guarantee that the spouse/partner is cheating, but is often a signal that your significant other is looking for something other than what is already freely available. It's a first shot across the bow of a ship on unsteady seas. Somebody is bored, in need of attention and wanting something to change.

But with investigation, comes opposition. Many a disgruntled spouse or vilified employee had decided that the only way to show their ingratitude was with physical confrontation. Ray and Barney were more than able to deal with such issues. Both were capable and loyal to the other; another reason for their success in business.

However, one case, in the previous year, had almost destroyed the business.

When Nina Fuller had walked into Ray's office and asked him to investigate the suicide of her brother, Daniel, it seemed pretty clear cut.

Ray looked at the evidence and thought that the case would be over before it began. Everything pointed to an open and shut suicide. He investigated just to be thorough, but soon uncovered a secret life that Daniel Fuller had hidden from his much younger sister all of her life; a secret life that involved a covert project, funded by the CIA, that researched into the possible military applications of psychic phenomena.

The story had all the makings of a conspiracy theory, an X-file or a documentary laced with dubious science and over-imaginative characters. Nevertheless, the story was true.

A collection of brilliant and powerful minds, whose unique gifts, had made them targets long after the project had come to a close, led to those individuals being dispatched in unimaginable ways; a trail of tragic events, shattering lives, culminating in one night, nearly ending the agency forever. Some of the scars from that night had healed, some never would. So colossal was the impact of the media frenzy that followed, damaging the business in so many ways, but also highlighting that there was no case the team would not take. The story made the national newspapers and several international ones. Ray's favourite headline was 'PSYCHICS USED AS HUMAN WEAPONS,' it was sensationalist but accurate. Luckily the business survived. Luckier still Ray, Barney and Nina also survived. Others were not so fortunate.

Ray also earned himself a very personal bonus. Nina Fuller went from client, to business partner, and eventually, life partner. The storm had been weathered and now the future looked positive.

However, Ray never lost sight that another case could come, and do similar, if not worse damage. He did not anticipate that such a case was right around the corner.

# Chapter Three

The unwelcome rain fell hard against the dirty pavements. It was the kind of rain that penetrated through clothing quickly if it was not waterproof. The uncomfortable chill breached his several layers easily. Spook huddled at the edge of the alley but the narrow opening offered little protection against the downpour.

Spook, real name Jamie Delaney, was homeless and scared. He lived on the streets of Croydon, a hostile place for an outsider at the best of times, but for somebody as vulnerable as Spook, it was terrifying. There were no family members looking for him, as he had no family and had been in the system since birth. With a mother too young to keep a baby, she decided to leave her new born infant son on the steps of the local hospital and walked away; never to be found.

After years of being passed from foster home to foster home, Spook ended up in an institute for children with behavioural problems but his problem was also his biggest asset. He was gifted in ways which very few were and others would never understand.

That gift got him noticed, pulled out of the system and into a very privileged position. But it was a position he did not want or thought he deserved. After more than a decade of living in the bright sunshine of Los Angeles, he escaped back to the UK and onto the streets, where he felt far more at home than he ever did living an affluent Californian life. He would always look out of place somewhere where looks were scrutinised to the nth degree.

He had earned the nickname Spook because of his gaunt expression. Large, deep set brown eyes with tight pale skin stretched over his long face and high cheek bones. His hair was a dirty blonde mess, often too long but currently very long, as he had been homeless for almost a year. He stood out in a crowd, towering above many. With his shoulders hunched, he still had to duck under doors, and even at a height of nearly six foot seven, he weighed very little. His body was painfully thin and undernourished, more so of late because of the lack of food available to him. Standing out in the homeless community made him an easy target. All he ever wanted to be was invisible.

As the rain seemed to ease, he made a move from the alley and headed toward the town centre. It was late and some of the restaurants would be emptying their waste food into the bins - the perfect opportunity for some kind of meal, so long as he could beat the rats to it. Some nights he would eat like a king but most would be slim pickings and a mush of scrapings dumped into the same waste bags. Roast beef and custard, chicken curry and cheese cake; beggars couldn't be choosers and that was exactly what he was; a beggar.

He ran across the road, avoiding the still very busy traffic of the town centre. Most of the vehicles were taxis or minibuses ferrying people to and from events, often in the not-so-far away London city centre. He had tried begging in London but found it too daunting a place. Too much violent competition, too many people looking to take advantage of a loner like him. Many thought him to be a teenage kid just trying his luck in the big city but the truth was he was twenty seven years old but looked so much younger, adding to his vulnerability and increasing the size of the target on his back.

The rain had stopped completely now but there was a squishing noise with each step he took with his left foot. A small hole had developed in his well-worn army style boots, letting water seep into the sole only to be forced out with every other step. It completed the unintentionally pathetic look he had achieved. His ripped, dirty black skinny jeans were soaking wet and clung tight to his giraffe like legs. Two thick black hoodies, over several T-shirts made up his top half, and a child's Spiderman baseball cap completed the ensemble. The look of a young vagrant wasn't easy to master.

He headed along one of his usual back alleys haunts, where a Chinese restaurant and a Mexican place discarded waste and would often provide some of the more decent grub.

As usual, Spook had his head down, not really looking where he was going and did not see the trouble up ahead. And when he did it was too late to run.

Had he engaged his psychic ability before stepping into the alley, he may have avoided what was about to happen.

"Hey! Skinny boy! Where you going?" A young sportswear clad yob, flanked by two other similarly dressed goons, stood in the middle of the alley, blocking the path.

Spook did not speak he merely stopped walking and raised his eyes to look upon his aggressors.

"What's up, bruv, cat got your tongue?" The words were spat with malice.

"Please…" It was the only word Spook uttered before the hands of sportswear yob were on him.

The yob reached up and grabbed Spook by his soaking hoodie and shoved him backwards. Spook looked down at the youth. He towered over his assailant but still did not lift his hands in any kind of defence.

"Don't..." Spook tried to talk again but was interrupted by a punch to the face. He had anticipated the blow yet did nothing to stop it.

"You're in my alley," the youth scowled, "and you have to pay."

"I don't have any money." A complete sentence escaped the psychic's lips this time.

"I don't like it when people don't pay, do I lads?" The two other goons grunted an affirmative answer in unison.

"Don't do this." Spook knew what would happen next.

"Do what? You're making me do this by coming into my alley without the necessary funds. I don't want to but I have to. I have a reputation to live up to, you know." The thug said in a mock sympathetic tone.

"Don't pull the knife." Spook said firmly.

"You're a smart guy ain't you?" True enough sportswear yob pulled out a lock knife from his trouser pocket.

With the knife held in his right hand, the attacker drew back his hand as if to lunge forward but the stabbing action that should have followed didn't.

Spook stood rigid with his eyes trained on the now frozen young man. It was as though time had stood still.

"Joe?" one of the flanking cronies uttered in confusion, "what's wrong?"

The head goon did not answer. He remained motionless, barely breathing. His glazed lifeless eyes stared into the distance, seeing nothing.

"What's up?" The other one offered. He put his hand on his friend's shoulder, as though to try and wake him from whatever trance he had fallen into, but that was a mistake.

Sportswear yob turned swiftly and sank the knife deep into the stomach of his concerned friend. The goon collapsed, clutching his wound, blood flowing between panicked fingers.

"What the Fuck?" the other goon shouted, as he tried to grab for the knife but again this too was a mistake. Sportswear yob span on his heels and caught his other companion in the ribs, piercing a lung, and again dropping the youth to the cold, wet alley floor.

With his two comrades incapacitated, the lone belligerent twisted toward the tall skinny man before him. Although it was not the younger man's will turning him on the spot. He was under the control of a force he could never understand.

The now pitiful looking young yob raised his left arm and rotated his forearm so his hand was palm up. In a single swift action the blade sank deep into his wrist. The youth squealed and fell to his knees as all control returned to his mind and body.

"I told you not to pull the knife." Spook uttered as he turned and walked away from the three injured thugs, leaving the leader of the group staring at the blade rising from the centre of his wrist, wondering how the hell it had gotten there.

Spook continued walking as the rain began to fall again. He would have to find some other place to eat tonight.

# Chapter Four

Ray climbed the steps to the first floor office space the agency operated from. There had been some renovation of the business, over the last few weeks, to give the office a more professional look. And even though there had not been any redecoration in the last seven days, the smell of fresh paint still hung in the air. Marge, the office manager, had bought a dozen air fresheners which had been placed on every desk and on every window sill to try and combat the odour. It had not helped.

"Morning Raymond," Marge greeted. "I trust you have been taking care of yourself in Nina's absence."

Marge was the mother hen of the office, looking after Ray and Barney, plus the office juniors, when it was needed and even when it was not. Every Friday, she would bring in either a cake she had made or treats from the bakery. As Nina was away on business, Ray had been left to fend for himself over the weekend. He was expecting some home cooked meals, prepared in plastic storage boxes, to be taken home and reheated - Marge was good like that.

"There has been an endless supply of take away food and manly DVDs to keep me entertained," Ray joked.

"Well, I've brought in some food for you," Bingo! There it was, "they're in a carrier bag in the fridge. Just pop them in the microwave when you need to."

"Thank you Marjory." He felt obliged to call her by her full name, as it was what she would bestow on everyone else, "I see Barney has a client."

In the far office, Barney's large frame could be seen, sitting across the desk from a very unhappy looking, balding gentleman in a grey suit.

"Michael has been in there for a while," Marge was the only person to call Barney by his real name - even his own teenage daughter called him 'Barney', "The client was on the doorstep this morning - probably trying to get in before work."

"Indeed." Ray agreed, "Any calls?"

"You have a client on their way in," she lifted a post-it note from off the desk, "A Mr Hogarth. An American, I think."

"Did he say what the case was?" Ray examined the name and mobile phone number on the scrap of yellow paper.

"He didn't say, but he did say that he only wanted to speak to you."

"Ok, send him straight in when he gets here." Ray made his way to his office, via the coffee machine. He hoped the smell of the fresh beans would kill the odour of week old paint.

As he dropped into his brand new, not yet worn in office seat, he observed the man in the suit heading for the exit. Barney was also out of his office and walking over to see his business partner.

"Morning gorgeous, is the bed too big now you are all alone?" Barney was all about the sympathy.

"Of course not, I've a stream of supermodels trying to keep me company," Ray jested.

"Jesus! These paint fumes must be getting to you."

"Nice! What's the deal with the client? He looked like a suspicious husband to me." Ray was not often wrong.

"A textbook case, the guy already has some evidence but no smoking gun as yet, he wants us to follow her and put in some coverts." Coverts were how Barney described micro spy cameras.

"What's his basis?"

"The wife has become very secretive about her whereabouts and is guarding her phone. She often goes on clothes shopping trips and always with the same friend. Also, she shows her husband the fruits of the trip, every time. But, a month or so ago, she went on one of her 'trips'," Barney made the air quotation marks as he said it, "and the husband bumped into the friend in the city on the same day. When the wife got home there wasn't much to show for that trip. He also caught her deleting messages off her phone. When he asked what she was doing, she said 'just making room' as her memory was getting full, but later that day he checked her phone, when she was in the shower, and there was at least twelve months of network provider messages, plus mundane texts to and from him, asking to fetch milk or a loaf of bread, stuff like that. If you are going to delete messages to create room, you would lose those first. She also has new underwear which he has never seen before and like I said, she shows him everything she buys."

"What do you reckon?" Ray asked.

"The wife is ten years younger than him and she looks ten years younger than her age. He on the other hand is no Johnny Depp. You know the score. The grass always looks greener on the other side but it's only greener cos it's fed with more bullshit. She's probably had her head turned by a younger guy who's only gonna stick around while it's still exciting and then move on once he's bored, or she wants to get serious." Barney was nothing but cynical when it came to love and romance. It was probably why he had been single for the last six years.

"Ok, let's get on it." Ray said.

"I think it's one for you. It's more your bag than mine." Barney was right.

"Well, I've got a client on the way in, and depending on what the case is, I may have to hand it over for Pete to do."

Pete was the office junior, the tech guy that every office needed. A pure thoroughbred caffeine fuelled geek.

As Ray finished talking he could see Marge leading a man toward his office.

"I'll leave you to it." Barney walked back to his own office, greeting the new client as he passed.

Marge walked in and made the introduction.

"This is Mr Bradley Hogarth."

The man, in his mid-thirties, extended his hand to meet Ray's.

"Please, call me Brad, Mr Dean," he had the kind of voice you might hear on an infomercial for car wax broadcasted in the early hours of the morning; crystal clear and louder than it needed to be. He was a Mr average otherwise, average height and build, with black hair, dark eyes and a tanned complexion. Ray suspected Hogarth had at least one Latino relative down the line from the colour of the man's skin. There were also a few crow's feet at the corner of his eyes where he had clearly been squinting against the sun whilst enjoying it. The man looked like he might have been a typical preppy college boy a decade or more ago - He still had a leather satchel bag over his shoulder as though he would be attending class. Ray felt sure that if he looked inside he would find an apple for the teacher and some peanut butter and Jello sandwiches, with the crusts cut off, neatly placed in the satchel.

"Ray, please." Ray also preferred a less formal address and gestured toward the chair opposite him.

The man sat, placing the satchel upon his lap.

"Coffee or Tea?" Marge asked out of courtesy but the man declined with a wave of his hand.

She nodded and left the room, closing the door behind her.

"What can I do for you, Mr Hogarth?" Ray rolled his eyes. He had been told to call the man Brad but still referred to him by his formal title.

"Brad, please." The man smiled but came across as quite emotionless.

"Sorry. Ok, Brad, what can I do to help you?"

"I need you to find somebody for me," Hogarth explained, "someone that does not want to be found."

"Well that could be a problem but we have been successful in such cases before. Do you have any details for me?"

Hogarth reached into his bag and pulled out a photograph and a folded sheet of A4 paper. The photograph showed a beautiful young woman; Olive complexion and jet black hair, longer than shoulder length and naturally wavy. Her eyes were also jet black, like dolls eyes. She was definitely a very exotic looking woman. Ray thought it would be difficult for someone with those looks to stay unnoticed for long.

Ray unfolded the sheet of paper to read the details.

The woman was called Roxana Petrescu, twenty nine years old, originally from Romania, an orphan with no known living relatives. As with other American clients Ray had encountered looking for a missing person, Hogarth had supplied height and weight also. Roxana was five feet three inches tall and weighed one hundred and ten pounds. The details were specific but necessary.

"Ok, Brad, why do you need to find her?" Ray asked.

"Is that relevant?"

"Very. If she is missing and doesn't want to be found then there has to be a reason why. You could have something illicit planned for this obviously beautiful woman. I need to know that we won't be putting her in harm's way."

"Trust me, Mr Dean. Sorry, Ray." Hogarth rolled his eyes the same way as Ray had, "Miss Petrescu is more than capable of taking care of herself. I am more likely to be in danger from her than she is from me."

Ray paused to digest that sentence.

"Is she in some kind of trouble?" he asked.

"Let's just say she has done some harm and needs to be located for her own good." Hogarth was not smiling anymore, not that his smile was in anyway comforting to begin with.

"I need you to tell me what she has done." Ray was firm. His smile was also absent.

Hogarth reached into his satchel once more and pulled out of a copy of the LA Times, dropping it onto the desk. A post-it note marked a page.

Ray opened the newspaper to the marked page and skim read the article. It was the reported death of successful businessman, and philanthropist, James Shriver, by apparent suicide. The details stated that the man had thrown himself from an overpass onto the fast moving lane of the LA freeway.

"This is a suicide. How is she involved in this?" Ray asked. His face frowned in confusion.

Reaching into the bag again, Hogarth pulled out another newspaper.

"You, of all people, should know that sometimes a suicide is not a suicide." Hogarth dropped the newspaper on top of the opened LA Times. The front cover of the year old Bristol Post said it all. There was no need for Ray to read this article.

SUICIDE HORROR AT HIGH STREET HOTEL.

The report referred to the death of Nina's brother, Daniel.

Daniel had been killed by means that Ray did not fully comprehend himself. And it was even more difficult to explain without it sounding like a story plucked from a book of the weird and supernatural, or from the pages of a conspiracy theory document. The murder weapon was the mind of a man, controlling another's mind to do harm. In this case, to make a murder look like a suicide, but there was not just one case discovered; three suspicious suicides, in three different locations, but too close together to be more than just coincidence. The story was extraordinary to say the least.

"What are you suggesting here?" Ray asked cautiously.

"I know you are familiar with the term Mindsweeper."

"I am."

"That is what Roxana is, a Mindsweeper. But from a new breed." Hogarth declared.

His blood froze at Hogarth's disclosure.

The legacy of a cold war project had not died twelve months ago, as Ray had hoped. Would the horror have to be relived again? The possibility was too much to contemplate. The thought of a younger, more motivated Mindsweeper was not only incredible, but terrifying too. Ray's heart pounded from adrenaline coursing through his veins, as the horror from more than a year ago burned to his very core.

# Chapter Five

Vincent Roux strolled toward the escalators. He loved flying, whether as a pilot or as passenger, it mattered little. He especially liked flying from Charles De Gaulle airport. It was akin to a mini space age city; the enclosed escalators and conveyor belts criss-crossing each other, bringing the various passengers to different levels of the airport. Most of his time would be spent drinking coffee under the huge glass ceiling of the gallery while waiting to board.

Currently he needed to use the bathroom and headed downstairs so he could also pick up a book or magazine to read on the flight. Los Angeles airport, or LAX as it was often referred too, always seemed too far a destination for a business meeting but with the future of his company that hanging in the balance, Roux felt it necessary.

Roux L'aeronautique was only a small development and research company, but it did hold the patent on a revolutionary design for a new type of wing, the GravEx.

The GravEx was shorter, stronger and could handle significantly more extreme G force manoeuvres from agile aircraft; but the real bonus was it was cheap to produce.

The meeting was to form a merger with a giant American company, SAED - pronounced Say-ED by those in the business. Roux was meeting with his Los Angeles lawyer tomorrow to discuss the finer points of the merger, to then engage in significant negotiations with all the partners of SAED and thrash out a deal. Roux wanted to maintain the majority share in his company and thus hold the patent for the design, plus the control of its applications. Companies would pay billions to use the technology for military purposes. Giant companies like Lockheed Martin and Boeing were ready to swoop in to create the next generation of military drones. The deal would make Roux a billionaire.

He stopped briefly at a magazine stand to peruse the latest gadget mags. Occasionally, he had been included in several articles, internationally, with his company being tagged 'The One to Watch' in Forbes and part of the 'New Generation Pioneers of The Twenty First Century' in Time Magazine. Roux had had the list in Time, framed, as he appeared only two places behind Mark Zuckerberg. He wasn't sure whether he was prouder of that accolade or the genius of his invention.

Out of the corner of his eye, he could see a man browsing at one of the other magazine stands. The man was flicking through the pages but was not looking at the magazine. The man's piercing eyes were trained directly on Roux, almost boring through him.

Roux was used to being followed, and one time, was attacked. Rival companies would pay handsomely for his personal laptop, to see if there were any new developments in the pipeline that could be copied and passed off as a new, unique design.

Roux was ex-French Airforce and had had military combat training. He could handle himself but decided it would be better to try and vanish, and not engaging in any confrontation if at all possible. Nothing was worth jeopardising the meeting in LA for. Pride and bravado would just have to wait for another day.

Swiftly, he made his way along the wide walkway, heading for the toilet block at the far side of the complex. His flight was not for another ninety minutes, so he could afford the time to lose the tail.

As he crossed to the other side of the main gallery, he looked back. The man had not moved but was still looking in his direction. Roux continued walking past the first toilet block, toward the next one, further along the gallery. Another cursory glance over his shoulder the man hadn't moved, and was still standing by the magazine rack but this time was looking at the pages of the magazine in his hands.

Breathing a sigh of relief, Roux laughed at himself for being over cautious.

He pushed open the door to the toilet block, stepping through into a large spacious room, with a row of urinals on one side, stalls on the other, and the basins running down the middle.

He walked up to a basin and ran the cold faucet. The water felt good against his skin - the fine sweat on his brow needed to be washed away. As he stood looking at his own reflection, he mused on the next international magazine article about him. 'A BILLIONAIRE BY FORTY' flashed across his mind. He laughed at his good fortune, forged from his own tenacious nature and intellect, before leaning forward into the basin once more, splashing more water onto his face.

As he rose, away from the porcelain, his reflection was no longer alone. A young blonde man in a suit had appeared behind him.

    "Can I help you?" Roux said in English whilst turning to face the man.

The man did not answer. He launched himself at Roux, punching him to the ground. Roux tried to get to his feet but was completely unprepared for the attack. The man kicked him in the face, sending Roux flying back into one of the stalls. Dazed, there was no answer to the attack. The young, clearly very strong, man, repeatedly punched the Frenchman in the face until he was unconscious. Without pause, the man bore down with all his might, forcing his hands against Roux's throat. The position was held until the helpless man stopped breathing.

The attack was over swiftly. The French Entrepreneur was dead.

The young man stood up, grabbed his briefcase and left the toilet block, walking toward the terminal, as any other passenger would.

The man at the magazine stand looked on, as the young man strolled passed him. In an instant, the man released his mental grip. The young man stopped in his tracks, looking around, clearly perturbed by why he was in a different part of the airport than he remembered being in.

Clad in a very sharp, expensive suit, Andreas Carling looked down at his right hand. The skin was broken and bruised, as though he had been in a fight. What had just happened to him? A glance at his watch told him he had lost about ten minutes of his life.

As Andreas stood pondering his confusing situation, the man at the magazine stand merely placed the publication in his hand back onto the stand and walked away.

Why make it look like a suicide when it is easier to make it look like a murder? This was how the man thought. This is how the man worked. And they called him Ghost.

# Chapter Six

Ray sat silently for a moment, his mind raced with the possibilities of what harm he and his colleagues could come to by taking this case. The broken mind of an elderly man nearly killed his entire team. What could a frightened young woman with self-preservation as her primary goal be capable of?

"What do you know of Mindsweeper?" Ray asked the American.

Hogarth hesitated, clearly contemplating his response.

He presumed either the man knew very little, hoping that Ray would fill in the blanks, or that Hogarth knew far more than he would be prepared to admit to and was selecting how much information he dared to give.

"I know very little," Hogarth started, "I've read the articles and checked out a few things on the internet. I heard the term Mindsweeper and looked it up. Your name was linked in a few websites. I actually read all about what happened with you and your team, on a conspiracy theorist blog. The claim was that you know how to catch and kill these individuals."

"The reports are exaggerated. Just because a spotty kid, who never leaves his bedroom, thinks I'm some kind of psychic whisperer, does not make it true."

"I'm not saying it is true but you have experience in these matters." Hogarth was deadpan, no emotion.

"Inexperience you mean. Inexperience cost two people a night in the hospital and two others their lives. I'm a private investigator, NOT a psychic catcher."

Hogarth took a breath before his next comment.

"What I am saying is that you were able to locate the person responsible and end the series of events. The reports state that you personally saved Miss Fuller."

"Like I said, the reports are exaggerated." Ray was not enjoying this conversation.

"Maybe," Hogarth could sense the mood, "look, Ray, I've flown all the way from LA to see if you can locate this woman; a woman that could be responsible for a death. I'll pay you way over your rates just to find her. I don't want you to capture her or kill her, just find her."

Ray searched his mind for both pros and cons for this case, but it seemed as though there were only cons.

"What is your connection to all of this?" he asked.

"James Shriver was my employer." Hogarth said it with no sign of grief, "I was his PA."

"Ok, what about the girl," Ray glance toward the sheet of paper, "this, Roxana? What is her connection to Mr Shriver?"

"My employer was involved in a lot of charity work. He was especially interested in helping orphans and disadvantaged children. Miss Petrescu was one of the children in a program set up in his name."

"He sounds like a good man." Ray said with empathy.

"He was, very good." Hogarth sat forward in his seat and locked eyes, "Look Ray, I know you must have some trepidation about taking this case but it will be very lucrative for you and your business."

"How so?"

"Whatever your rate for this job, I will pay double - treble if need be."

"I charge by the hour," Ray said glibly.

"I'll pay you three times your hourly rate, twenty-four hours a day, seven days a week until you find her." Hogarth said sternly, "I will even pay you a month in advance to prove how much I want your services. And if you find her tomorrow you can keep all the cash."

Ray mulled over the offer for a moment. As much as he wanted the business, he was pretty sure it was not worth the risk. Had he learned enough from the mistakes of the past? He wasn't sure. But if he took the case he may make the same mistakes again and probably some new ones.

"I'll have to discuss this with my partner."

"Very good," Hogarth was up on his feet instantly, dropping a business card onto the desk, "my cell number and e-mail address are on the card. I'm staying in the city, so I can return for further discussions if you wish."

"Ok, Brad, I'll be in touch." Ray stood and offered his hand.

"Nice to meet you Mr Dean," Hogarth shook on it.

"Where are you staying in town, by the way?" Ray asked out of courtesy in a vain attempt to lighten the heavy atmosphere.

"The Grand."

"The where?" Ray knew what he heard.

The Grand Hotel was the scene of Daniel Fuller's death, also where Daniel's killer tried to repeat the act with Nina. That event would live on, deep within the memories of all those involved in that night. The whole saga of The Mindsweeper started at that hotel, and now this stranger, who had come to hire Ray to send him back into that nightmare, was staying there.

"The Grand," Hogarth could see the effect his answer had had on the investigator, "I thought I might have a sense of connection if I stayed there."

"But of course." Ray opened the door and ushered the man out, "I'll be in touch."

Hogarth merely nodded a response and left.

Ray kept his eyes trained on the American until he had disappeared through the reception entrance.

As he turned to go back into his office, to contemplate potentially the most dangerous case of his life, Ray caught sight of Barney looking across from his office doorway.

"You look like you've seen a ghost," Barney offered to his obviously perturbed colleague.

"Worse, in fact," was all Ray could muster.

He ambled over to Barney's office to have a conversation he really did not want to have but there was no time like the present.

# Chapter Seven

1990 - Romania.

Claire Cooper brushed the dust from her jeans and opened the door to the visitor she had been waiting for. There was a brief introduction but she could see that the man was eager to conclude the business he had flown so far to conduct. She directed him into the building and closed the heavy wooden door.

The building was old and in a very poor state of repair. Dilapidated was not a strong enough word to describe a structure that was little more than a shell that had been patched repeatedly; so much that the patching was most of what now remained. Wood blocks from the parquet floor were missing and crudely replaced with cement to level the floor. Damp had stripped off almost all of the wallpaper, exposing the rotten plaster, and most of the paint work had been chipped back to the wood revealing the dry rot and woodworm. The building was as sorry looking as its purpose.

Walking the gloomy central corridor, the visitor glancing through door-less frames to see almost exactly the same scene in each room they passed. Inside were bedrooms, overcrowded with makeshift cots, most of them touching. In each cot was a child, usually crying. Ages varied from a few months, up to eight years old. All wore ill-fitting clothes, all had their heads shaved, to prevent lice, and all were malnourished. It was the biggest orphanage outside of Bucharest.

The wailing of the children drowned out any possible chance of conversation between Claire and the visitor. It did not matter for there was no need for small talk. She wanted the man to leave as soon as he had paid her. $5000 US dollars for a phone call seemed like a good deal to her. It would pay for a flight back to the states and set her up in an apartment. She had had her fill of humanitarian work, longing for a regular job with a steady wage in a familiar country.

She was leading the man upstairs, deeper into the building, to one of the smaller rooms toward the back of the rundown establishment. With each step, the musty air thickened. So much so that there was a taste that came with the stench. The cold mildew mixed with the smell of urine, excrement and vomit, compounded the building's desperate existence. It seemed hard to believe that this was a functioning building.

The final corridor twisted left and then right. With no natural light to show the way, a few low power light bulbs had been haphazardly strung from the exposed wooden ceiling. The dangling loops of wire hung low so low that they had to be avoided rather than ducked under.

The sound of a hundred crying children dissipated somewhat but never completely disappeared. But there was no noise from these rooms, all of them were empty; and for good reason. This part of the orphanage needed to be isolated.

At the very end of the windowless passageway was *the* room.

Unlike the many other rooms they had passed, this one had a door in the frame. Not only was the door closed but it was also locked. Claire pulled out a small bunch of keys and slid the largest of the keys, a skeleton key, into the lock. It took some effort but eventually the key turned, the lock grinded and the door was unlocked.

She opened it to reveal a very different room than the others.

Although also in a poor state of repair, this room had pictures on the walls.

Hand drawn pictures of faraway places, were thumb tacked to the few remaining slabs of broken plaster; it was the handiwork of a very young child.

Tucked into one corner, near to the only window, was a single metal framed bed. Stained sheets were pulled to one side and a grubby flattened pillow lay at one end. It was far from an inviting place to sleep.

As they entered the room Claire spoke in Romanian.

"It's OK. You can come out. We're not here to hurt you." Claire did not know the man's objective but thought she would try and reassure the room's only occupant.

But there was no sound.

The man, who had said very little since arriving, crouched down and peered under the bed.

"Hi, little one," he said in English in a deep American accent.

"She doesn't speak Eng…" Claire's words were cut off.

"I think she can understand me. If she is as you described, then she has no need for words." He gazed into the void under the rusted, old bed.

A grubby, sad expression came into view. Long jet black hair straggled over the face of a young girl. Her eyes were as black as her hair. She crawled forward then stopped, brave enough to be seen but not brave enough to leave the safety of her hiding place.

"You can understand me can't you?" The man asked.

The little girl slowly nodded.

"How?" The perplexed Claire asked.

The little girl only ever spoke in Romanian and never very much of it.

"Tell me about the pictures," the man asked Claire, ignoring her question, "Tell me about this one."

He plucked a sheet of A4 off the wall. Drawn in green crayon, was an image of a figure with an arm raised into the air.

Claire gazed at the scrawl.

"I was talking about home and she drew that picture."

"Where are you from?" the man asked.

"New York,"

"So this must be the Statue of Liberty?"

"I believe it is," Claire did not know what it meant but it scared her.

"Did you show her a picture of it?"

"No."

Across the wall were so many images. A yellow cab, the Brooklyn Bridge and the Manhattan Skyline, dominated by the twin towers of The World Trade Centre - all drawn with the uncoordinated hand of a child, but clearly recognisable for what they were.

The man turned his attention back to the space under the bed.

"So then little one, how would you like to come with me?" He smiled, "There are others like you. But I think you will be most special."

The child crawled further from under the bed. She knew that he spoke the truth. She knew everything he had in store for her. Young as she was, little Roxana knew the man offered her a better life than the one available in her own country. She could see the warm summer skies of his world through his memories. It seemed a magical place, to someone that had only known the cold damp existence of a meagre orphanage.

"How old is she?" The man asked.

"Four," Claire answered but as she looked toward the girl, she could see the child had extended four fingers already.

The man took her hand, gently easing her from her hiding place.

"Come little Roxana, I have some friends who you'll want to meet." He led the child from the room.

Little Roxana left the orphanage, and the country that day; never to return.

# Chapter Eight

There was no debate. There was no argument. There was only an agreement. They would not take the case.

"It would be crazy to take it, regardless of the money," Barney said.

"So we are completely in agreement? We will not take this case?" Ray did not want to seem like he was overruling his partner.

"Definitely! Nina would flip out if we took it. Are you going to tell her?"

"I guess I'll have to," he knew it was the right thing to do, "but I'll wait until she's back home."

The last thing he wanted to do was to upset the woman he loved when she was a thousand miles away on a business trip, although breaking the news to her in person was going to be hard enough. Ray could not even comprehend how he was going to tell her. *'Oh, you remember last year, when you nearly died when a psychic assassin tried to kill us all? Well somebody has asked us to take on a much deadlier case, with more risk, and more variables.'* It wouldn't be an easy conversation.

Ray mused to himself that the news alone might trigger a flashback or something similar. Even once the threat had been eliminated, Nina had suffered for months afterwards.

The Mindsweeper had placed what was known as an anchor into her subconscious while she slept. The anchor was similar to a backdoor password on a piece of software. It would lay dormant until such time as the Mindsweeper would activate it to gain control of the subject with ease at any time, accessing the subject's memories or controlling all motor function at will.

Although there was no longer a Mindsweeper to activate the anchor, Nina still had difficulty falling asleep because sleep was where the attacks started, when a subject is at their most vulnerable. Even if she did sleep, often she would wake in an anxious state; reliving the nightmare events of that night.

Saying 'no' to the case was easy, saying 'yes' was not an option.

Ray stood, about to go back to his office but his thoughts wandered toward what to do next. He needed to focus on something other than Hogarth and his lucrative offer.

"I can look at the suspicious husband case for you, if you want?" Ray asked his partner.

"It's more your thing than mine," Barney said handing Ray his notes, "It will also keep you occupied while your lady is in Spain."

"Ain't that the truth," Ray laughed as he took the notes and headed back to his office.

He dropped the paper onto his desk and settled into his chair. The agency revamp had meant giving everyone a new high backed office chair. He didn't like it. He much preferred his old leather swivel chair.

As he wriggled in the seat trying to find a comfortable spot, the phone rang.

"Hello, Barnett & Dean," he gave the official response in his best telephone voice.

"Hello, I'm looking for a man," the female voice said.

"Any man in particular?" Ray asked.

"A good looking man. Maybe a Michael Fassbender look-a-like with an aversion to organisation and tidiness. I need help to find a way out of my boredom. Do you know of such a man?" The voice said playfully.

"I think I know the very man. He looks more like the doorman from hell than an 'A' list celebrity and has limited social skills. He answers to the name of 'Barney'," Ray laughed down the phone.

"Oh my god Ray, anything but that," Nina laughed back.

"Is it that bad out there?" Ray asked.

"I'm so bored that I'm thinking of jumping on the next flight back home," although Nina was in Spain, it was a business trip to buy a nightclub, a bar, and a restaurant. She was in Puerto Banus, the playground of Spain's rich and famous but she always loathed the place, if the trip was business related.

Nina was a beautiful woman and a shrewd business operator but when dealing with the older Spanish businessmen, she was treated as just a dumb girl in a man's world. It was something that she was not used to because she was anything but dumb..

"Do it!" Ray said, "Marge has made me so much food, I must look pathetic without you around."

"You look pathetic with me there," she joked.

"Thanks for that," he took that one on the chin, "you'll be ok once you've charmed Pedro,"

"It's Pablo," she scolded.

"Surely that's an Italian name," Ray questioned.

"And mine's Russian and the most Russian thing I do is drink too much vodka,"

"True," Ray could never beat her on banter once she got going.

"Look, I just wanted to phone and say that I missed you and can't wait to get home to see you." she was being sincere, another thing she was very good at.

"I miss you too," Ray's voice was hushed. He hated soppy talk down the phone. The thought of telling her about Hogarth's visit flashed across his mind but was eradicated with her next statement.

"I love you,"

"I love you too," he replied.

"I have to go now. I'll call you tomorrow when the deal is done."

As quick as that, she had hung up. Ray worked hard to keep Nina interested in him but he didn't need to, Nina wasn't going anywhere soon, at least not of her own free will.

# Chapter Nine

Croydon town centre was heaving with afternoon sunshine shoppers. The weather was good and those without work were making the most of blue skies and warmth. The pedestrianised area rarely saw so many people, the cafés had put their summer tables and chairs back out to capitalise on the footfall. The pubs were doing even better trade as the Rugby World Cup had started that week and the glorious sunshine was perfect to bring out the Rugby fans, casual or otherwise. Today: Wales versus England. The match wasn't kicking off until later that day but every drinking establishment in Croydon, with a large screen television, was already packed.

Roxana fought her way through the crowds but it was not easy. Not wanting to take the chance of being seen, she had decided to wear Islamic dress as a disguise, dressing head to toe in long black garments and a burqa to cover her face; but it created a whole other problem.

With some many large groups of men, fuelled with alcohol and prejudice, the atmosphere around her was hostile. Only some things were said out loud but she did not need words to be spoken to understand what people were thinking. Her mind was an open receiver to all thoughts directed toward her. A Mindsweeper's gift was to hear the thoughts of others - but some thoughts she would have rather not heard.

> *'It's our country, they should dress our way'*

> *'Fucking Muslims'*

> *'I bet she could do with a real man to take that off her'*

> *'Pretty eyes, shame I can't see her tits'*

A tsunami of racist and sexually motivated insults overwhelmed her. No matter how swiftly she moved the torrent abuse could not be outrun.

Ducking down an alley between two shops, she hoped that disappearing from view would make the voices in her head stop. But she would not be that lucky.

The comments steadily slowed down but somewhere out of view, her attire had sparked heated debates that would echo for some time to come.

She had slowed her pace but, halfway down the alley, she realised she was not alone. Two men, one young, one middle aged, were relieving themselves in the alley after several early pints.

She had not seen them, as they had tucked themselves into a doorway. Even though she was psychic it was impossible to know everything that was happening around her. The white noise caused by the racial discussions, she had accidentally instigated, had clouded her mental vision making her vulnerable.

"Whoa, shweetheart where d'you think you're going?" The older man slurred his words as he stepped into Roxana's path.

She said nothing. She tried to sweep his mind but the alcohol swirling in his consciousness made it difficult, almost impenetrable. In her experience, a small percentage, one in million people maybe, were completely impenetrable, unreadable. Their minds were a closed book even to the most powerful and capable of Mindsweepers. This guy wasn't impenetrable, as she could access part of his brain, but the level of alcohol in his bloodstream was so high that he himself couldn't think straight, and that made it very difficult for a Mindsweeper to function within such compromised mind.

Although, Roxana did not have to read his mind to know what he was thinking. The darting of his eyes up and down her body, told her enough about this man's intentions.

"What's up love? You wearin' a gag under that thing?" The young man cut in. Pointing at the burqa and laughing. His mind was easily readable. The beer had kindled an unhealthy desire. Usually, Kyle; the younger man, would look for an equally inebriated young woman to take advantage of. But an opportunity had presented itself in the form of this small Muslim woman, or what he thought was a small Muslim woman.

She tried to back away but the older man reached out, catching her by the arm. His stance was unsteady but his grip was powerful. She could feel his fingers touching the bone. With his other hand he lifted the burqa to reveal what lay beneath.

"Wow! She's pretty, Jeff," said the young man revealing his friend's name.

"Isn't she just! You shouldn't wear this, love," said the older man, throwing the burqa onto the filthy alley floor, "you have pretty eyes and an even prettier mouth. I think you should show us what you can do with it."

He twisted her delicate arm in his vice-like callused hand, forcing her on to her knees.

Roxana would need to focus. She closed her eyes but not against the inevitable.

"Don't worry love this won't hurt," the older man unzipped his fly with his clumsy drunken free hand, releasing his penis.

The stench of fresh urine filled her nostrils as the man pulled her closer.

"I'll go first Kyle," Jeff said laughing at the power he had over the woman.

Kyle did not hear. Kyle did not see.

The older man thrust his hips toward the diminutive woman's face. She managed to turn her head but felt the damp tip of his semi erect phallus touch her cheek. The fear from within her sparked a reaction.

Suddenly, the younger man swung an arm, his fist catching his friend right in the centre of his face. The older man staggered back, releasing his grip on Roxana.

Kyle swung again but missed, throwing himself off balance. Jeff was the more physically able of the two, retaliating immediately. A swift left jab was followed by a perfectly landed right hook, knocking out his young friend.

Roxana's heart sank. Her only hope for escape was to use her power over the younger man, but she couldn't control anyone who had been rendered unconscious.

"What the fuck?" Jeff said at the passed out body of his friend and then turned his attention back to the woman, struggling to get to her feet.

Roxana had caught her shoe in the hem of the full length dress she had mistakenly chosen to wear. She was trapped.

"Looks like it's just you and me sweetheart," the older man had pure evil in the unfocused gaze of his eyes. A bead of blood descended from a nostril after the blow to the face. He wiped it away and returned to his evil intentions.

He grabbed hold of Roxana, by the neck, and thrust her into the corner of the doorway nearby. Try as she might, the man was too strong for her; physically and mentally. This was not going to happen, not if she could help it, but there was very little she could do to defend herself now; almighty in mind but fragile in body.

The man pushed his knees into her chest, pinning her to the door, so he could use both hands to unfasten his belt, lowering his jeans. Reaching out, he took hold of her head. Roxana closed her eyes and forced her mouth shut in her final desperate attempt to prevent the violation that was about to be perpetrated upon her.

Suddenly, the grip on her head released. She opened her eyes in time to see the older man fall back onto the alleyway, trousers around his knees, unconscious.

"You're lucky I knew where you were," Spook's large sorrowful eyes stared down at the wretched sight of a friend in so much despair. He reached out, helping her to her feet.

The tears ran down her face as she leapt into his arms. She did not need to express her gratitude out loud. He knew how thankful she was. They were the same. As their bodies embraced, so did their minds.

"How?" the question popped into her head and the word instantly escaped her lips. In her head she was asking how he had overpowered the man that meant to harm her.

Spook held up a house brick and then promptly dropped it to the alley floor.

"Let's get out of here," he said, fearing that either of the assailants could be back on their feet soon.

The pair hurried out of the alley, their hands entwined. Together again after what had seemed like an eternity. Separately they were powerful, but together they were formidable. And they needed to be, for they knew the lengths that others would go to in order to find them.

# Chapter Ten

Ray slumped into the large soft sofa of the penthouse apartment he shared with Nina. A steaming mug of tea and a bacon sandwich sat on the coffee table, next to a newspaper with greasy finger marks lining the edges. Reading the paper, whilst grilling the bacon, had proved to be a messy task but Ray wasn't bothered. He was fending for himself, his beloved was out of the country and a little mess was allowed.

Somewhere beneath the paper, his phone vibrated. The number was withheld. Even with a mouth full of sandwich, he took the call.

"Hello. Ray Dean." he answered.

"Mr Dean," Hogarth's drawl was unmistakable, "You never called me back."

"I'm sorry, Mr Hogarth," the earlier first name agreement discarded, "I have been rather tied up with another case…"

"Surely, my lucrative offer should take priority. Do you not think so?" Hogarth interrupted.

"Not really Mr Hogarth," Ray was annoyed, "Your case might get me killed, so I was going to call and decline your offer."

"Mr Dean," Hogarth mirrored the annoyance, "I am not asking you to stalk the country chasing a young lady with a butterfly net. I wish for you to merely locate Miss Petrescu, nothing more."

Ray considered his response. He was not one to be dictated to but he also did not wish to sound ungrateful for the potential business he was disregarding.

"I understand that, but I think the risk is far too great for me, and my people. I have every right to decline the case and that is what I plan to do. I wish you luck in your quest for Miss Petrescu but my firm will not be involved."

"I am deeply saddened by your response Mr Dean, but I have to respect your decision. If I was to increase my offer wou…" Hogarth's proposal was cut short.

"There is no amount of money that would change my mind. I'm sorry Mr Hogarth."

"So am I, Mr Dean, so am I," there was no goodbye. The line went dead.

A bemused Ray tossed his phone onto the sofa and reached for his sandwich again. As he bit down, the screen lit up and the phone vibrated on the soft cushion of the sofa. It was Nina.

"Hey you," Ray struggled to talk with the amount of bread, ketchup and bacon that he had tried to force into his mouth.

"Hi, my lovely," Nina's voice never sounded so good, "have I caught you eating?"

"Don't worry about it. At least you know I'm being fed," he joked, spitting crumbs everywhere.

They talked at length about their respective days at work, although Ray omitted the meeting and subsequent phone conversation with Hogarth. While it was always a blessing for Ray to listen to her positive, upbeat voice telling him all the things he longed to hear, occasionally she would deliver some bad news.

This time she would have to stay in Spain, for an extra two days, while the business was halted because of a hitch. The hitch being that Pablo, who she was buying a business from, could not pay his solicitor. He clearly had a cash flow problem which was the reason for him selling his club. But he also had a delay in the funds being transferred from one of his offshore accounts, or at least, that was the story. Whether it was true or not changed nothing. She would be spending another forty eight hours away from Ray. He felt lost when she eventually hung up.

Absence makes the heart grow fonder but Ray could not fit any more into his heart, not when it came to Nina. He had never felt so much for another person before. She had turned his whole life around and given him so much more than he could have ever had dreamed of. He was so grateful for her presence and often doubted whether he could return everything that she had done for him. His love for her was limitless, he hoped it was enough.

As much as he would miss her, there was nothing he could do about her absence. He took a moment to think about more practical ways in which he could fill his time. A weekend without Nina would mean he could squeeze in some work to fill the time but he knew that Barney might try to take advantage of the situation and drag Ray out for a long overdue boy's night out.

After much consideration, about five seconds of it, a night out might be a good thing. He grabbed the phone and punched Barney's number. If they were going to have a boy's night out then at least it would be Ray's idea for once.

\*

Hogarth did not need to dial a number to get the message across. Within a minute of hanging up from Ray Dean, his phone rang.

"He's not going to do it is he?" the voice said.

"No he's not but you knew that already," Hogarth answered, "you know what comes next?"

"I'll book a flight as soon as I get off the phone,"

"Have you had any success at all?" It was the question Hogarth had to ask.

"She doesn't want to be found so she won't be found," the voice answered, "she can't remain hidden indefinitely but I think she may have help."

Hogarth mused on the information for a moment.

"Spook?" Hogarth asked the question but he already knew the answer.

"Most probably."

"That will make her more dangerous and us more vulnerable," Hogarth said.

"Only you or I are at risk. Raymond Dean on the other hand is quite safe," the voice said.

"Ok. Do it!"

"I'll ring you once I've landed." The voice rang off.

He had guessed that persuading Ray would be difficult. Ray's skills would have to be employed, at any length.

Hogarth knew things that Ray did not. He knew that Ray was an impenetrable. Ray could not be controlled or read by a Mindsweeper, regardless of how powerful they were.

In the quest for Roxana, Ray Dean was the key. His services would be acquired, regardless of the cost, or the incentive.

# Chapter Eleven

Her eyes flickered open against the light that crept in through a gap in the curtains. It took a while before she knew where she was. The room was so unfamiliar, so different than what she was used to.

Roxana sat up and stretched her arms, taking in the rest of the strange surroundings. The hotel room was basic and functional, more importantly, it was anonymous and warm.

She gazed toward the bed on the other side of the room. The covers were missing from and there was no occupant. She couldn't see him but she could hear Spook, breathing as he slept somewhere else in the room.

Carefully stepping out of the bed, she tiptoed through the discarded items on the floor between the beds. Spook had literally stripped where he was standing and dropped most of what he was wearing, before taking a shower the previous night.

Sure enough, he was curled up under a duvet on the carpet next to the wall. She smiled a sad smile. Spook had started the night in the bed but through his time on the streets clearly it was more familiar for him to sleep on a much firmer surface.

Roxana watched his eyes dancing beneath eyelids. The dream sleep had him deep within its clutches and not letting him go anytime soon. As his breathing became more erratic, his body started to spasm. The dream that enveloped him was not a pleasant place to be.

Sitting on the edge of the vacant bed, she closed her eyes. Entering Spook's mind would be the only way to understand his dream. The link was easy, as it had been made before, many times, usually under duress, but this time Roxana penetrated the young man's mind freely.

\*

She found herself on a cold, black, wet street, somewhere within an unidentifiable city. The buildings were oppressively tall. So tall that they punctured the dense black clouds that filled the sky. Everything was black or a shade of dark grey. There was no colour. Even the rain that fell vigorously against her skin was black, like soot filled dank water plummeting from the heavens. The only light came from antique street lamps. There were no bulbs in them, just a dull whitish grey flame, not unlike old gas street lighting of the 19$^{th}$ century.

As she walked along the dirty pavements, Roxana swiftly realised that she was barefoot. A jagged stone dug into the sole of her foot. She dropped down on to the high curb, adorned in nothing but a short, black dress to examine her injured foot. Blood oozed from the small wound, even that was as black as pitch.

Suddenly, somewhere in the distance, there was a scream. Not a woman's scream, but a man's; a cry so desperate that it filled the air with a piteous essence, echoing from one of the many alleyways the led from the street.

Her injured foot forgotten, Roxana got to her feet and headed toward the sound, it had now changed from a scream to a groan. As she flitted from one side of the road to the other, searching for the source of the noise, the groaning lessened. She stopped walking and spun on the spot, trying to determine which alley would be the correct one.

Boldly, she walked into the nearest chasm-like entrance to an alley, peering into the blackness. The sound had now lessened to nothing more than a whimper. Without the volume of a scream, it was increasingly difficult for her to pinpoint which way was right and which was wrong but she pressed on, stepping into the blackness, regardless.

As her eyes adjusted to the dark, she could make out the shape of old metal dustbins lining the walls of the alley. Rubbish spilled out onto the worn cobbles, where large black, filth caked rats gnawed on fleshy bones, thankfully ignoring the barefoot intruder that had wandered into their domain.

As she shuffled her way through the debris covered path, careful not to disturb the feasting rodents, a loud scream pierced the blackness once more. The sound seemed to emanate from the very bricks of the buildings, as if the shadowy city screeched for mercy from the oppressive black downpour.

The scream made her bolt to the end of the alley, out into an almost identical street to the one she had first found herself on. The whimpering that followed the scream sounded so much closer but not enough to reveal the exact location of the stricken soul, the source of that wretched noise.

She entered another alley to discover that the scene was identical as the one she had just left; dustbins, rubbish, bones and rats. She ran over the cobbles this time and out the other end of the alley. She did not stop to take in the view of the street. She knew it would be the same.

Without pause, she ran across the empty, drenched street and back into alleyway opposite. It was the same.

She ran and ran, never seeming to tire, the scene never seeming to change. It was as though on a loop; an endless nightmare city without start or end.

She lost count of how many streets she had crossed or how many alleys she had entered when, without warning, another scream emitted from the bricks. So loud was the sound that the vibration knocked her off her feet, dropping her onto the cold wet cobbles, their icy touch impossible to bare.

Recovering from the deafening, malevolent noise, Roxana noticed that this alley was different. There was no exit to the street, just a solid brick wall that had no summit. There was a collection of dustbins up against this endless wall, with rats swarming over discarded rags that were strewn from a bin that had fallen over.

The whimpering came again, this time echoing out from the fallen dustbin. She almost screamed herself as she realised that the bundle of rags, where the rats swarmed, was the clothed body of her troubled friend.

Spook, huddled into a ball, protected his face from the countless vermin that bristled over his body.

She looked around for some kind of weapon to chase the rats away but there was nothing. She looked behind her. The alley had vanished. There was no longer a means of escape, only another brick wall, boxing her and her petrified friend into a roofless cell, where the black rain continued to fall.

With little regard for her own safety, she rushed in, kicking out at the vermin. The beasts squealed and shrieked, as her bare feet swiped them away. One by one, the rats were discharged, bursting into a cloud of thick dust and then disappearing forever.

With all her strength, she pulled at her friend, trying to free him from the dustbin he had wedged himself into. Slowly, the pathetic figure of Spook, inched his way from his shelter. Her words comforting, reassuring even, against contrast of the horrific dream sleep.

    "You're safe now," she uttered, "You're safe now. They can't hurt you. I've got you."

She hugged Spook's freezing, soaked form as hard as she could. Forcing her body against his, trying to ease the trembling of his limbs. But the ice that filled his muscles, seemed reluctant to leave, as though the nightmare was fighting for survival. Trying it's best to freeze out the angel that had willingly entered this vision of hell.

Slowly but surely, the quaking dissipated until the pair just held each other, sharing the warmth of mutual embrace.

She released Spook to gaze upon his sullen face. Grimy tracks rolled down his hollow cheeks into the wispy beard that barely covered his chin.

"It's going to be OK now," Roxana spoke softly, the subtle remnants of her Romanian accent seeping through into the American English she had spoken for most of her life. She waited for a spark of recognition from her friend's bottomless, black eyes.

Beyond the stunned silence, a flicker of normality glimmered somewhere deep within the sorrowful gaze of the desolate man before her, and she knew that he could be reached.

With her eyes closed, she took control. It was time to end this nightmare.

As she took a deep lungful of air, the rain instantly eased. She drifted into a trancelike state and started her own dream; a better dream.

Gradually, the soot filled water stopped falling. The black clouds broke up, rapidly changing to a pale grey, and eventually to white wisps that delicately veiled the bright blue sky beyond. It was the first burst of colour she had seen since entering Spook's traumatic nightmare.

The black bricks faded to bright red, the tar-like mortar that fused the walls of the roofless cell dissolved away. As though lighter than air, the bricks were carried away on a gentle breeze until no bricks remained.

There was no more rain filled city. The filthy black streets had been replaced by green meadows. Butterflies floated through the warm, comforting air. Flowers sprouted from the rich, lush grass at unnatural speeds. This was not natural at all. This was Roxana using her gift. Not in the way she had been trained to use it, but for the purpose she always thought it should be used for.

When she finally opened her eyes, there was no hint of oppression or fear, only warmth and joy.

They stood, holding hands, facing each other. Their clothes were no longer wet and sodden but light and dry. The black rags that Spook had been wearing were now comfortable hessian trousers and a cotton shirt. Roxana's black dress had been replaced with a white flower patterned gown.

Together, they turned toward a warming sun, which hung unnaturally large in a cloudless sky. They strolled hand in hand, as though the glowing ball of fire was their destination. The world they inhabited slowly faded out to bright white with each step they took and slowly, they were drawn back into their world.

*

Spook's eyes opened. He blinked against the reality of his surroundings, only just remembering he was in a hotel room.

Roxana, still perched on the end of the bed, smiled down at him.

"Morning," she said quietly.

"Morning," Spook shook his head as to evacuate the last remnants of the foul incubus that tried to cling to his mind. "And thank you."

"You're welcome, Jamie." She held out a hand.

Spook took it, feeling her squeeze his long pale fingers with her small tanned digits.

She had saved him from the nightmare. Now, she hoped that he could save her from the nightmare that pursued her, although, she would never be able to wake from hers. The nightmare she faced was the reality of her own ability and those who wished to exploit it, and so much more.

# Chapter Twelve

The evening still held heat from the day. Even with the sun now a dull and heading rapidly for the sanctuary of the horizon, it still felt like midday on a good British summer's day but without a breeze cooling the air.

Nina strolled alone along the Calle Ribera, on Puerto Banus' marina front. One side of the narrow road was lined with bars, cafes and restaurants, the other boasted a plethora of indecently expensive cars. Ferraris, Lamborghinis, Bentleys and Porsches, all parked up, herringbone fashion.

So many people doing the same as her, enjoying the bustling evening, that she did not notice the man following her.

He kept a distance but held the same pace. At any time he could have intruded into her vulnerable mind but chose not to. A quick mental scan revealed there was an anomaly.

Deep within her subconscious mind was an anchor. An anchor was a mental implant which facilitated how a Mindsweeper would take control of a subjects mind. While the subject was at their most defenceless, usually asleep, a Mindsweeper or a hive of

Mindsweepers, would implant the controlling thought. Once activated, the subject would be completely under the Mindsweeper's control and could be made to do anything, from a simple task, to something far more complex.

This man did not need to use anchors or be part of a hive. He was powerful enough on his own but then, so were most of the new breed.

Besides, entering a mind with an anchor already placed could be dangerous for the subject. She needed to be alive and well if she was to be of any use to them.

The closer to her apartment she got, the less people Nina encountered. With the sky now a burnt orange and the sun shining somewhere beyond the horizon the air finally started to cool. With just a few hundred yards to her apartment she decided to stop, sitting on one of the concrete blocks that lined the dockside to take in the beauty of the Mediterranean sunset.

Nina pulled out her phone and tapped on Ray's number. They hadn't spoken since yesterday as her business dealings had taken most of the day to complete. She had even been too busy to eat. Hungry and tired, she had walked straight into the first decent restaurant she came to after the meetings had ended. A bite to eat, accompanied by a glass or two of wine, had been well deserved before heading back to her apartment.

The phone went straight to answerphone. Either Ray was on the phone or out of the flat and in a poor signal area. He would never switch his phone off.

She placed the phone back into her handbag, sitting for a while longer, enjoying her surroundings for the first time since she landed.

Her work was so important to her but so was the free time away from the property dealings. And as beautiful as the harbour was this evening, it was tainted by Ray's absence.

Nina had always been independent and as much as she thought Ray needed her, she needed him more than she would ever admit. It seemed almost a lifetime ago that she had hired him to investigate her brother's death, and although very reluctant to do so, he took the case and committed to her, becoming more than just a client, she had felt the warmth of the man's character and the empathy he had for her situation. He had saved her life and in return she had saved Ray, from himself. Their mutual bond was equal and not as one-sided as Ray often believed.

She pushed the thoughts of Ray back and took in the view one last time. Various yachts and cruisers were lined up on the vast concrete jetties. Nina often dreamed of having one. It was not that she didn't have the money because she did, but it was the practicality of owning an ocean going cruiser and the fact that she was constantly busy trying to manage her multitude of properties and business ventures, to be able to spend the time jollying on a six figure extravagance such as a boat.

That pipe dream would have to wait until she retired, which was possible now but not what she would have wanted. She loved her work. The legacy she inherited from her brother had quadrupled her already successful property portfolio, making her a very wealthy woman, but she thought it would be disrespectful of her to sit idle and live off the profits. Nina would constantly strive for more as it was what her brother would have wanted.

With a subtle cool breeze now coming off the sea, she opted to head back to the apartment, take a shower and phone Ray later.

She stood, swinging the strap of her bag over her shoulder, turning back toward the direction which she had come from. A man loitered some twenty five metres away. He was not looking at her but his presence disturbed her. He seemed wrong – she couldn't put her finger on it but her gut feeling was always to be obeyed.

Setting off at a faster pace than she had previously been walking at, Nina hoped the pang of paranoia she was feeling was just that; paranoia.

Crossing the road that divided the marina from the apartment complex, she gave a cursory glance over her shoulder. The man was following and keeping pace.

Thinking it would be wise to try and lose him when she rounded the next corner, Nina would have to break into a sprint. She was a regular runner, very fast and very fit. Recently, her training had involved sprint training and even with a meal and some wine inside her, she felt confident to outpace most people over a short distance.

With the corner just a dozen metres away, she looked over her shoulder again to see the man had quickened his pace, closing the gap between them. She inwardly thanked her decision to wear soft lace up canvas shoes instead of strappy sandals. The canvases would be better to sprint in and Nina was sure she could get to the end to the narrow road she was approaching before the man could gain on her significantly.

Turning the corner was like a starting pistol releasing her. Nina slipped her handbag from her shoulder and swiftly wrapped the strap around her wrist before kicking her heels into top gear. She was many things, smart, beautiful and witty, but she was also quick on her toes and sped along the narrow pavement of the empty street like the seasoned runner she was.

From behind, she could hear the quickening steps of the man that followed but they were not close, which led her to believe that her hunch was right, she would outpace her pursuer.

She afforded a glimpse behind her as the end of the road was just a few paces away. Sure enough, the gap between her and the man had been significantly increased and he did not seem to be closing it any time soon.

With the soft glow of the street lights illuminating the junction, the apartment complex entrance was just metres away. Nina took her foot off the gas and slowed her sprint to a jog.

She reached into the handbag to retrieve her keys. The glance down at her bag was enough of a distraction for her not to notice the figure in the doorway just ahead.

The figure launched from the doorway, catching Nina by surprise. The short buzz of the Taser stung against her skin, completely disabling her. She fell into the figure's arms and was pulled off the street into the doorway.

Within seconds the pursuing man arrived breathlessly.

"What are you doing here?" the man was surprised and a little scared.

"Fixing what I knew you'd mess up, and you need to get fit," The figure said.

"I guess so," the pursuing man replied, "I usually don't have to chase them."

"She was too quick for you. You'll need help if you want to contain her."

"I don't need hel…" his retort was cut short.

"I'm not asking, I'm telling." The figure's said curtly.

"I've got some local assets so I'll see what I can do."

"Just do it. I haven't got time to bail you out again."

The pursuing man didn't speak again. Not that they needed to speak to communicate. The next part was simple enough and hopefully, Raymond Dean would see things their way and take the case. This was plan B and it was in motion.

# Chapter Thirteen

Too many bodies, too close together, that many people rammed into a confined space, was unpleasant to say the least. Condensation, generated from the breathing and perspiring crowd, slowly trickled down the papered walls. The moist, warm air, coupled with the cacophony of a hundred different conversations, made the room claustrophobic. He had to get outside, away from the noise and stale atmosphere.

As he stepped out of the hot pub, onto the cold street, the night air hit Ray like a sledgehammer. He stood for a moment, letting the breeze cleanse him of the grimy sweat that covered his body. The light cotton shirt he was wearing, beneath the heavy khaki jacket, seemed to unglue itself from his skin, making him feel human again.

There were very few people on the street, just a few stragglers, either heading for the next pub or making their way home.

Ray bounced on his toes, trying to get the blood flowing in his tired legs. He would have to wait for Barney, who had now stopped to talk to the guy that had collared them as they were about to leave. Barney liked to talk.

As he breathed in the fresh air, it felt as though all his drinks had been on standby, waiting to be uploaded to his cerebral cortex and the outside atmosphere had been the clearance code. He suddenly felt unsteady on his feet as the night's alcohol was delivered all at once.

Ray looked through the window to see that Barney was now deep in comfortable conversation.

He tapped the glass. No response. He tapped harder. Barney turned and waved a single finger at Ray through the window. It was assumed that he meant one minute and nothing else.

Sauntering up the street, he decided the walk might do him good and headed toward the taxi rank. A quick glance at his watch showed it to be just after midnight. It felt later. Maybe the lack of practice, or dare he think it, old age, was taking its toll.

Usually, Barney would have wanted to hit a club right about now, but instead, it was he that had wanted to leave. Ray was thankful that no club or restaurant had been suggested and looked forward to putting his feet up on the sofa, where he would fall asleep, probably.

With a head full of liquid euphoria, his thoughts focused in on Nina again and how much he was missing her. Before they decided to make a go of their relationship, she would often spend her free time jetting off to one corner of the globe or another, but that had all changed and now she would spend all her spare time in Bristol, waiting for Ray to finish his day's work. As haphazard as both their careers were, it seemed to work for them. They had more time together than apart, which was always good, but it made the void created by her foreign travel felt all the more.

Ray continued to wander up the street, with only his wistful thoughts for company. Looking back he saw that Barney was still nowhere to be seen and the pub was about fifty yards behind him now, it wouldn't be a surprise if another round of drinks had been bought, and Ray forgotten about. It had happened before and it was likely to happen again.

Approaching the taxi rank, he groaned, there were no taxis waiting for custom.

He perched himself on a low brick flower bed that was designed to decorate the urban landscape. Flower bed was a loose term, there was only a dozen or so flowers struggling to grow in the debris filled soil. He sat counting the rubbish, calculating there were more discarded soft drink cans and bottles than there were flowers.

Too busy observing the work of the unknown litter louts, he was completely unaware of the approaching footsteps.

"Hey man, you got a smoke?"

Ray turned his attention toward the voice. Standing before him were two men, both in their late twenties, one in jeans, a black sports jacket and a woollen hat, the other in black cargo pants and a dark hoody with the hood pulled up over his head.

"No, I quit a while back. I'm sorry guys," Ray answered.

"That's too bad," the voice belonged to the man with the hat, "maybe we'll just have to take your wallet and phone instead,"

"I beg your pardon?"

"You heard. Wallet and phone, now!" hat-man was now brandishing a knife, "that watch looks expensive. We'll take that too!"

Ray remained seated on the flower bed, glaring up at the men. It must have been obvious to them that he was not afraid. An exchange of confused glances between hat-man and hoody was the hesitation that showed their bravado was opportunistic rather than habitual.

"Look guys, why don't you just piss off! I'm tired, I'm drunk and I'm heading for home." Ray said in nonchalant defiance.

Hat-man lunged forward, not to stab but to appear more threatening, bringing the blade within inches of Ray's face. Hat-man was about to make his demands again but he did not get the chance.

Ray swiftly reached over the top of the man's arm with one hand and gripped hat-man's wrist from the bottom. In one rapid movement, he clasped his other hand underneath the wrist and twisted the man's hand over, forcing his arm straight. With a little pressure, the man dropped the knife and was brought to his knees. Ray could have easily broken his assailant's arm.

The hoody looked stunned and was resistant to respond. Eventually, he lunging forward, swinging a fist toward Ray's face.

Unable to dodge the punch, Ray took the impact square on the chin and was moved backwards by the force. The backward movement twisted hat-man's hand all the way over, dropping him face down on the pavement, Ray releasing his grip.

Hoody landed another, better punch, stunning him more than the first but Ray was still able to counter the blow with one of his own. Ray's right fist caught hoody cleanly on the cheekbone, breaking it with a snap. A left hook followed and that was all it took to reduce the hoody to an unconscious heap on the cold concrete floor.

Hat-man had recovered his knife but was obviously in pain from the twisting of his arm. This time he stayed at a safe distance to brandish the weapon. Ray could see that the man knew he was in some trouble. He could see the cogs turning in the hat-man's brain, weighing up the options and realising the mugging endeavour was a mistake.

"You're in a world of trouble now, ain't ya pal?" Ray said dabbing his lip from the second punch, realising that it had split, blood oozed from the corner of his mouth, "Do you want to try and rob me again without your wingman? Pick your friend up and go? Or just run for the hills? It's a tricky choice, I can imagine."

"Shut the fuck up!" the man danced about, the knife, a barrier between himself and Ray.

"Ok, I will, but all your troubles are behind you now,"

"Eh?" hat-man was confused by the statement. Not as confused as he was by the tapping on his shoulder.

Hat-man turned his head quickly to shoot a glance over his shoulder but he never saw the oversized fist coming.

Barney had snuck up and sparked out Ray's assailant with one punch. Hat-man fell, the unconscious body of his hooded friend breaking the fall.

"Thanks for that," Ray said casually.

"No problem. Now let's get the hell out of Dodge before the boys in blue turn up," Barney said, nodding toward a taxi that had just pulled in.

Ray agreed. The pair jumped into the minicab and headed home.

The conversation in the taxi was just the regular mundane chat that they had shared in the pub. No air time was given to the two would-be muggers who were probably just coming round about now.

As the taxi dropped him on the corner of his street, Ray bid his friend and colleague a good night. The only positive thing about the attempted mugging was that it had sobered him up significantly.

He tapped in his door code and was greeted by the security guard. Ray decided he would take the lift, as his tired legs did not fancy the five flights of stairs tonight. The alcohol, that still swirled within his grey matter made the swift ascent of the lift feel exaggerated and the halt more sudden.

The lift door bonged as it slid open to reveal his front door. Ray did not step out of the lift immediately.

There was a letter taped to his front door.

Cautiously, he stepped forward and touched the envelope. There was something small and solid inside. He pulled the tape from the door and opened the letter.

The solid item was an SD card, like those found in a digital camera. It was wrapped inside a single piece of A4 paper which had a brief message neatly printed in blue ballpoint pen.

He read and reread the words, not because he did not understand, but because he did not want believe what the message was telling him. He was suddenly very sober and for the first time in long while, he was scared; very scared.

# Chapter Fourteen

Her eyes opened, wide, in the unfamiliar room. Nina lifted her head from the pillow and took in her surroundings.

A plain white bedroom, quite large, with a table and four chairs in one corner, a sofa in another and a wall mounted TV facing the foot of the bed. There was also a large sliding glass door leading to a balcony to her right. The view beyond was of the marina area of Puerto Banus illuminated against the black night but from a more highly elevated position than she was used to viewing.

As she tried to swing her legs off the bed, a sharp pain in her ankles stopped her movement. She looked down to see two pairs of handcuffs, a set secured to each ankle and the heavy cast iron bed frame. She sat up. The adrenaline flowed freely as panic set in. Where was she?

With both hands wrapped around one cuff, she pulled with all the strength she could muster. The frame groaned but it did not give. A quick scan of the room for any available tools revealed nothing obvious. There were two doors on opposite sides of the room, one probably to the bathroom and the other to a lounge area maybe, she had no clue which was which but maybe one held the key to her freedom.

In answer to her question, the door facing her opened and the man that had been following her walked in from what looked like a lounge area. In the light of the room she was able to see that he was about thirty, give or take a year, average height and build, with tanned olive skin, shaggy black hair and pale green eyes; whatever threat the man was on the streets, seemed to have diminished, surprisingly.

"Hello, Miss Fuller," he spoke with a subtle Eastern European accent; Polish maybe.

Nina said nothing. She froze and tried to make it look like she was not attempting to break the cuffs.

"I'm sorry for this inconvenience but it is necessary at this time," the man smiled. His smile was warm and his apology sounded sincere. Not what she was expecting at all but then it was not an everyday occurrence to be abducted from the streets of Spain.

"Why are you doing this?" she asked with no expectation of an honest answer.

"I know that it is not what you want to hear but you have been taken as an incentive."

"Pardon me?"

"It is confusing, I know. You wish to escape but there are no tools in the bathroom for you to use. It would be better for all concerned if you just sit tight, let things take their course and you will soon be on your way." The man had real empathy in his eyes.

"What 'incentive'? What are you talking about?" Nina felt able to ask the question even though she felt she was in no position to do so.

"I know you have many questions but I will tell you things as you need to know them. I shall bring you some water but you should really try to sleep. Your rest is very important." The man said, again with a smile.

She almost smiled back, as though the cuffs or incarceration did not exist for a moment. She nearly said thank you but held back her words, not wishing to sound too compliant to this strange man.

"You are welcome," said the man with a chuckle in his voice.

Nina's confused look said all she needed to say. How had the man answered the statement she had refused to utter?

"Listen, you should get some sleep and we will talk in the morning," he chuckled again.

"Who are you?" she asked, not expecting an answer.

"My name is Jakub, I am a Mindsweeper, but they call me Ghost," he said the words knowing that she would understand. He could read every thought and nuance that her subconscious mind would generate.

The full horror of her situation hit her harder than the Taser that had stunned her into unconsciousness. The jeopardy she found herself in was overwhelming. Regardless of how polite and agreeable the man appeared to be.

She, like Ray, had thought the Mindsweepers had died more than a year ago, with Edward Langston, her brother Daniel, and the last two remaining Cold War Mindsweepers. If the programme still existed, with younger psychics, and kidnap was an acceptable part of the project, God only knows what these people were capable of.

# Chapter Fifteen

Just thirty minutes after parting company they were back together at the apartment.

Barney seemed unduly sombre to Ray. He was usually so upbeat and positive about any situation, or could at least come up with an alternative solution or a sarcastic gem. Instead he had nothing.

Ray had nothing either, just an abyss in his soul where all thoughts of Nina should be.

They went into the office. The video from the SD card was paused on the screen of a laptop. It showed Nina unconscious on a large white bed, her ankles cuffed to the bedstead. Ray clicked 'play' and let the clip run. It was fourteen seconds of footage recorded on a mobile phone. Whoever filmed it merely walked around the bed and showed Nina's face in close up.

There was no conversation between the men as yet. The images spoke enough, telling them things they did not want to see or hear. The only exchange between the pair, since the envelope had been discovered, was the panicked phone call Ray had made as soon as he entered the apartment.

He handed Barney the note.

*'I THINK THIS WILL MAKE YOU RECONSIDER MY OFFER. I WILL CALL AT YOUR OFFICE AT 9AM ON SUNDAY MORNING. DO NOT INVOLVE THE POLICE OR YOU WILL NEVER SEE MISS FULLER AGAIN.'*

Barney placed the note on the desk.

"This Hogarth doesn't play by the rules does he," Barney said.

"No he doesn't." Ray stared at his friend, "What do you suggest, because I got nothing."

"Have you tried ringing her to see if this is genuine?"

"Both apartment and mobile - no answer on either," Ray's face was ashen as though he had aged thirty years in thirty minutes.

Barney could empathise.

Ray was a very different man a year ago or so ago. He was a heavy drinker and smoker, who lived on takeaways and microwave meals. Although a keen investigator, it was the job that had given him enough focus to make it through the days. Without the agency, Ray Dean would have had a completely different existence. Nina had entered his life, rocked his world and shook him out of his chaotic lifestyle. He was fitter, leaner and more determined than Barney had ever seen before. But without her, the downward spiral would be rapid, probably sinking to depths that even Ray had never fallen to before.

"Take the meeting and see what he wants. If we have to, we'll take the case." Barney said very matter-of-fact.

"I don't want to take the case. The last time we dealt with these people Nina almost died, Pete was put in hospital and Casey…well you know what happened to Casey."

On that night, just over a year ago, the whole agency had been on a stakeout. There was a Mindsweeper hunting down Nina, and Edward Langston, a member of the original Mindsweeper project, funded by the CIA back in the 1970s. The same project that Daniel, Nina's brother, was involved in because he too was a Mindsweeper. The project collapsed after just five years of research and those who had survived intact, more or less, went back to their lives. Whilst they were already gifted in the ways of psychic phenomena, the project had honed their skills and given them more control over their powers.

There were originally six men in the project – Manny Sanchez, Edward Langston, Daniel Fuller, Bruce Graham, James Vaughan and Tom Ryan - but Ryan, the youngest of the participants, took his own life when an experiment with Sanchez, the head Mindsweeper, went very wrong.

Sanchez wanted the project to continue but his success pivoted on the input of the others, and with great effort, he drew them all in for one last experiment. Again, it went disastrously wrong. The others managed to escape, relatively unharmed, except for Langston and Sanchez.

As the two most powerful Mindsweepers from the project, they created a single consciousness to dwell in. Their individual powers did not merge well, causing the link to collapse catastrophically. Langston's mind was damaged, but Sanchez' had his erased, or so it seemed.

Without the top dog, the project was halted. Langston eventually recovered and lived as a recluse in the depths of rural Wales. The others went back to their lives, using the powers they had developed for their own needs but never to cause harm. The remaining participants probably would have made it in to old age had it not been for one critical event.

Langston had a stroke in the summer of 2014, releasing the genie from the bottle. Sanchez' mind had not been erased - it had simply found refuge in the chasm that was Langston's brilliant brain. Sanchez had been locked away in a metaphoric cell somewhere, hidden deep within the part of the brain where Langston's power resided. The stroke had smashed the walls down on that cell, forcing Langston to use the part of his brain where his psychic ability resided. Two conscious minds lived as one within a single brain. Langston was unaware of Sanchez' presence, but Sanchez knew exactly where he had been living for thirty years and took sweet revenge on the other members of HIS Mindsweeper project. Daniel Fuller, Bruce Graham and James Vaughan were all killed in staged suicides. Langston, on the other hand, could not be killed as Sanchez would have perished with him.

The whole agency was brought in to keep an eye on Nina and Langston, as they were most likely the next targets and used as bait to draw out the Mindsweeper. But nobody could have ever guessed the assailant was already under surveillance. With everyone in close proximity it was easy for the disembodied mind of Sanchez to run amok.

While Langston slept, Sanchez activated an anchor he had previously embedded in Nina's mind, for her to kill herself at all costs and anyone who tried to stop her. Once she was in motion, Sanchez took control of the mind of a young security guard, attacking Barney and Pete, who were watching Langston. The attack was halted when the security guard was killed in a collision with a taxi. Barney was injured and Pete spent the night in hospital with a hairline fracture to the skull.

Casey was not so lucky. She had been tasked with looking after Nina at a local hotel and had had to give chase when Nina tried to leave the hotel.

Nina attacked Casey with a fire extinguisher, breaking her nose, gashing her forehead and knocking her unconscious. Although she recovered, Casey could not be in the same room as Nina for very long. It was understandable and regrettable but she left the agency.

The last Ray had heard was that the formerly bright and bubbly, would-be actress, Casey had become reclusive and was receiving therapy after a suicide attempt. She had more scars on the inside than would ever be visible on the outside. They had all been very fond of Casey, hating how this had affected her.

Nina had also suffered long after the event, Ray did not want any kind of repeat.

"Ray," Barney was brainstorming, "we need to know much more about this Hogarth fella and what he's into."

"I know that. What are you suggesting?" Ray snapped back.

"The guy is clearly well motivated, well connected, and rich. He could use anybody to hunt down this girl but there must be a reason that he wants to use you. We're gonna have to dig into everything about this guy."

"So?" Ray's mind was not able to function beyond how on earth he was going to save the woman he loved.

"You look for this Roxana girl, ok? And I will look into Hogarth,"

"Ok. Who gets Pete?" There was often a tussle over who would be able to use their very resourceful tech guy.

"I do," Barney smiled even though there was nothing amusing about the situation, "I need him to find Nina."

"And how is he going to do that?"

Barney leaned into the laptop and popped out the SD card.

"Well he can start here," Barney said brandishing the digital memory card.

"And what am I going to do?" Ray asked.

Barney looked at his watch. The time had crept up to nearly 2am.

"Your meeting is in seven hours. Get some sleep, if you can, but if not, get your head straight and I'll meet you at the office, Ok?"

"Ok," It was as much as Ray could muster as his head swirled with uncertainty.

"Good, I'm going to wake Pete up now and get a head start. I'll bring breakfast, you just bring yourself,"

Without another word Barney was gone.

As the door slammed, he turned back toward his laptop and placed his hand upon the screen where Nina's image had just been. He was fearful. Fearful for her but allowed himself the greater share of his fear. Never before would he have to rely so heavily on his team. He knew they would never let her down, but Ray was doubtful how well he would perform. He would have to wing it, just like in the days before Nina.

# Chapter Sixteen

After a day and a night of laying low in the hotel, Roxana knew they would have to move on. Their reservation had not been booked in the traditional sense and their occupation of the room would soon be discovered. Her main concern was to get Spook out of his dirty clothes, get him washed, fed and into some new clean clothes. She would use as much of her ability as she dared to meet those needs and keep the pair of them safe and warm for 48 hours or so.

Two days earlier, just before her run in with the two drunks in the alley off the main Croydon thoroughfare, Roxana had linked mentally with a hotel receptionist, controlling the woman, who had just started her shift, to book two nights full board on a major corporate account. When she returned with Spook a few hours later, laden with food and a change of clothes, they booked into the room. The receptionist had asked for ID from both of them. Roxana had asked if a driving license was ok and when she was told that was fine, she merely held up her empty hand, the receptionist nodding her acceptance of the identification.

Spook's grubby hand was also identification enough.

Such was Roxana's ability, if she wanted anyone to think they were being chased by a lion then someone would be running for their lives with nothing more than a psychic's simple thought pursuing them.

Two days was as much as they dared to get away with. Sure, Roxana could probably link with another member of staff and get a few more days but every time she used her ability it made her vulnerable. Opening up her mental pathways acted like a beacon to others like her. If she continually used her powers then they would soon be found. It was only because of this weakness that Spook was able to locate her when she was attacked in the alley and tried linking with one of her assailants, it drew attention. Thank god it did.

The weakness, if it was a weakness, was something that people with a psychic ability had to deal with. Their minds were always open and able to receive any mental information from others, whether others had ability or not. It was, after all, called Extra Sensory Perception, and they were always perceptive.

The so-called scientific experts on psychic phenomena put people into a particular category based on their individual abilities. Almost every person had some degree of psychic ability, most not recognising it within themselves or wanting to expand it.

At the bottom of the food chain were the intuitive, those that were able to feel a situation, but little more than that. They took the feelings as hunches or gut feeling, even without thinking it could be more. The intuitive class were vast and made up almost a quarter the earth's population. On the hypothetical scale of psychic ability from one to a hundred, the intuitive fell between four and eight.

Next were the sensitives. These were people with ability to feel and read the emotional attachments that others have with one another. This class was made up with those who were stage magicians, spiritual healers, and psychic mediums such was the connection to other people. Some mediums, that gave very accurate readings about deceased relatives to bereaved folk, were merely sensing the thoughts of the bereaved and interpreting the information as though from 'the other side.' There were others that actually read all relatives, dead or alive, connected to an individual, and thus telling the paying customer facts that they did not know but later investigated and found to be true. The psychic mediums did not know where or how they received the information but often passed it on as 'messages' from the deceased, bringing great comfort to many. Although, some of the psychic mediums disregarded this theory, stating that spirit guides led them to the information. The experts would argue this point, the truth was that neither the psychics nor the experts could prove the other wrong as the theory could never be confirmed, only measured. The sensitives accounted for about five percent of the population. The range of ability varied, from very intuitive to intensely sensitive. The measured range for a sensitive was between nine and twenty five on the scale.

The remote viewers were special. These were classed as the crème-del-a-crème of psychics. A range on the scale from twenty six percent up to sixty five percent, their abilities varied considerably, but that ability could be measured more accurately and confirmed through constant testing. These were the psychics that were used by both the KGB and the CIA during the cold war for the purpose of spying, or psychic infiltration, as some referred to it. It was through the creation of Project Stargate that the discovery of very powerful psychics was made.

The military application for the use of psychics had to be given a name. The head of this side project to Stargate, Marcus Harrison, initially trialled the psychics for counter espionage and mental reconnaissance. One or more of the psychics in the project were brought in for some security scenarios. To see if they could scan a room or a building for possible threats, bombs or even insurgents. Harrison made reference to his father, who was a captain of a Minesweeper in the Second World War. He said that his father's ship was of the utmost importance and that it cleared the way, protecting the battleships and aircraft carriers allowing them to do their jobs. The side project became known as Mindsweeper. The psychics were sent in as part of a secret service detail to clear the way and protect any VIPs in situations that were considered high risk. Instead of sweeping the water looking for potentially dangerous mines, the operatives swept the crowds or buildings, looking for dangerous minds. It was a tongue in cheek play on words but the name stuck and anyone with a very high extra sensory perception score from Project Stargate was thrust into Project Mindsweeper. Only those with a psychic ranking of over ninety five percent were considered the elite known as The Mindsweepers. There were only six in the original programme and that was enough. They were all male and all six were now dead.

Roxana was of the new breed of Mindsweeper. She was the only female to ever score beyond the required ninety five percent. Her score was off the chart, so high that it could not be recorded, making her the most Powerful of her kind.

Powerful meant valuable to those who seek such extraordinary talents, and those that did, had unlimited resources and showed no compassion or remorse.

# Chapter Seventeen

Ray arrived at the agency early - too early. The clock on the dashboard read 7:18. Tucked into the corner of the carpark was Pete's battered, blue Vauxhall Astra. He figured Barney must have been true to his word and did indeed wake Pete to get him started on the investigation.

Truth be told, Ray could have been there sooner but there had been much pacing of the flat and wallowing in a pit of anxiety to get through first. At least he had plenty of time to clear the alcohol fog from his mind with an unhealthy amount of coffee. He did wonder if the alcohol fog was the only thing that protected his mind from much of his anxiety, keeping his brain ticking over. Whatever it was keeping him going, he was hoping for some news to bolster the shattered remnants of his spirit.

The stairs up to the office never seemed as high as they did today. Ray's legs felt heavy, from a run he had been on a few days ago, coupled with the quantity of alcohol that had entered his system on the previous night. Today would be the longest of days.

The atmosphere in the agency felt heavy and oppressive. Nothing was different, except for Ray's perception. For him there was no spark; no feeling of belonging; no Nina at the end of a phone waiting for him to start work. Every day from hereon, would be different, regardless of what had happened to Nina. She could be delivered back to the agency with a bow around her and a bouquet of flowers but Ray now knew what it would feel like to lose her and how powerless he was to prevent it.

Ray walked into the main office to see Pete working away at his laptop, head down with his fingers dancing across the keyboard, like a concert pianist lost to the melody. There were four Red Bull cans on the desk, three were crushed, one was intact, which most likely meant it still had liquid in it.

"Morning sweetheart," Barney surprised Ray by stepping out of the staffroom with a mug of coffee gripped in his large fingers. He was still dressed in the same clothes as when he had left Ray.

"Morning," Ray said taken aback, "have you been here all night?"

"Yes," Pete cried without looking up from his screen.

"I think he was talking to me, Pete," Barney said, "yes, we have but we may as well have not bothered."

"You've got nothing?" Ray looked toward their tech expert.

"Nothing of any significance," Pete said, "the clip was filmed on a Samsung mobile phone and a geo tag put the clip in Puerto Banus which is nothing we don't know."

"Well, she's still in Spain, should I book a flight?" he looked at Barney for approval.

"The clip is ten hours old, Ray," Barney could see the desperation in his business partner's eyes, "I don't want to say it, but she could anywhere by now."

Ray knew he was right.

The situation was destroying Ray from the inside out; he needed to get a grip. It was no good taking a wild stab in the dark, it was time for clear thought, but clear thought was obscured by the image of Nina, lost and alone.

"I know, I know," he did not need to say what was going on in his head, his colleagues knew.

He fixed himself a cup of coffee, then sat with his equally tired looking colleagues. They discussed the whole night from the message being stuck to the door to the moment Ray walked in. There was no denying it; they had very little.

When Barney had left the flat, the first thing he did was approach the security guard for the building, asking him what had happened. The guard reported that nothing unusual had happened at all but when reviewing the CCTV footage there was an anomaly. All the cameras had been switched off for about seven minutes, more than enough time for someone to get into the building, tape the envelope to the door and escape. When tackled about it, the guard swore blind that he was not a part of anything. Barney could see at the time that the guard was genuinely confused but seemed truthful. With the type of people they were dealing with, anything was possible, so he took it no further.

"So what's the Plan?" Ray didn't feel that he could make any rational decisions, leaving Barney to make a judgement call on how to play the situation.

"Take the meeting, we'll record the conversation and you just keep the guy talking." Barney talked like it was just another case, not letting Nina's involvement sway any decision he would normally make.

"Apart from where the fuck is Nina, I don't think I'll be asking him much more. What do you want me to say?"

"Ask him as much as you can about this Roxana and that James Shriver guy. We need to know as much as we can before we start a search but we need all the background on this Shriver. And you need to stay cool. I know you, Ray. You'll want to smash his face in but he's the one in control. He has Nina and you have to play his game in order to get her back."

"I get it," Ray was not dumb but he could sense that Barney was telling him things like he didn't have a clue, "dig deep, get him to spill his guts and don't smash his face in."

"Exactly that" Barney nodded.

\*

The time seemed to drag by but eventually Hogarth entered the building. This time he was not alone. The American had brought two burly minders with him. One was young, in his twenties maybe, but larger than Barney. He had thick muscular arms, protruding from an undersized polo shirt, covered to the wrists in tattoos. The other man was late thirties/early forties, short, stocky, with a nose flattened unnaturally in the centre of his face, just like a boxer.

"Good morning, Mr Dean. Or should I just call you, Ray?" Hogarth afforded a wry smile letting them know who was in control.

"I don't want you to call me anything. I just want to know where Nina is." Ray contained his rage. He wanted to pound his fists through Hogarth's smug face until he broke through to the back of his skull. The two additions to the American's entourage were no deterrent. Ray just wanted Nina back safely, physical confrontation, whilst satisfying, would not meet that end.

"She's fine and won't come to any harm provided you cooperate with my request"

"Then you need to start talking and answer EVERY question I ask," Ray demanded.

"Certainly," Hogarth smiled "shall we go into your office?"

There was no reply. Ray merely gestured toward the room. The entourage entered. Ray followed the men with Barney bringing up the rear.

The office seemed claustrophobic with so much testosterone situated between its four walls.

Hogarth sat in the chair, as he had the previous day, but this time with his minders flanking him. Ray took his seat while Barney perched on the edge of the desk.

"Firstly, why do you need ME to find this Roxana?"

"Why NOT you, Mr Dean? You found Langston, a Mindsweeper that didn't want to be found - I think you'll be perfect," Hogarth mused.

"You are clearly well-funded and organised. You probably have far more resources at your disposal than we do and so it begs the question 'Why me?'"

"You're correct. I am well-funded but I chose you for a reason, one which you may not be aware of. We have tried other avenues and all have failed so far. You are the man to find her. Of that, there is no doubt in my mind."

"We could go round in circles here," Barney cut in, "just tell us what you know about the girl and the guy she is supposed to have killed."

"You are direct aren't you, Mr Barnett, or should I call you Barney?"

"My clients call me Mr Barnett, my friends call me Barney, but you're neither shithead, so cut to the chase, spill the beans and get the fuck out of our office before your two new boyfriends have to take you to a bone Doctor." Barney's voice never altered, even when he delivered a threat, it was part of his menace when he used to be a Police officer.

The two burly men shifted uncomfortably but never spoke.

"Well, if you put it like that," Hogarth disregarded the threat, "I'll start at the beginning."

Hogarth did indeed spill his guts. Roxana was an orphan of Romanian descent, this they already knew, and had been taken to the USA via one of Shriver's children's charities when she was just four years old. Stating that he was not sure why she had been singled out but her psychic ability was the most obvious reason and she was entered into a research program for gifted children, again this program was funded by one of Shriver's many charities.

Although most of her childhood was supported by Shriver, Roxana did not meet her benefactor until she reached her 21$^{st}$ birthday. Apparently, Shriver liked to throw a coming of age party for his 'Children', as he called them, and setting up employment and an apartment to further support those from less fortunate backgrounds.

Roxana had worked in the fund raising department for Shriver's main charity for eight years, until disappearing without a trace.

 A week later, Shriver takes his jump onto the freeway; Roxana being the main suspect.

"That is pretty thin!" Ray uttered.

"What do you mean?" Hogarth replied.

"You have nothing. No evidence. No knowledge of what has happened to this woman. How have you come to this conclusion?" Ray asked.

"Ray's right, this is bullshit!" Barney interjected, "Maybe Shriver killed the girl and topped himself through guilt. There's your case, open and shut! If you've any better theories we're all ears."

"The girl is not dead," Hogarth stated firmly.

"How do you know?" Barney asked.

"We just do,"

"This is bullshit. Shall we call the police now and tell them about your bullshit story, and your bullshit kidnapping plot?"

"THE GIRL IS ALIVE!" Hogarth screamed across the desk, "WE KNOW SHE IS!"

"Raise your voice in my office again and I'll kick all shades of shit out of you, and your hired muscle," Ray remained calm for once, "now there's a pile of info you're not telling us and you need to TELL US everything."

"Like what?" Hogarth spat.

"How do you know the girl is alive and why do you think she killed the old man," Barney butted in again.

"We used another like her," Hogarth said.

"Another like her – explain?" Ray questioned.

"Another Mindsweeper," Hogarth was trying to hold on to the details through gritted teeth, but if he wanted these men to cooperate with him, he was going to have to play ball, "we hired someone with the same ability to find her. He found her but she sensed him. She can switch off her ability, which renders her invisible to other Mindsweepers."

"If another Mindsweeper can't find her, how do you expect me to?" Ray said.

"Because she won't know you're looking for her." Hogarth's demeanour had returned to his normal sociopathic self.

"How do you figure that?" Ray asked.

"You are an impenetrable," Hogarth said it as though the detectives should know what he was talking about, "that's why I picked you!"

Ray and Barney cast each other a confused glance before looking back at the American. The details of this case were going from the bizarre to ridiculous. What else could possibly follow?

# Chapter Eighteen

The cheap curtains of the budget hotel barely held any respite from dawn's intrusion. First light tugged at the corner of her eyes, trying its best to awaken the sleeping psychic. She had already been disturbed and this was not the first time Roxana had been woken during the night. Spook had shrieked a piteous cry several hours earlier, prompting Roxana to enter his mind again to calm the demons that visited him nightly. She had to rid her own mind of the nightmare before sleep was possible, and although exhausting, the cleansing did not help her fall asleep any easier.

This time, her own mind had stirred her from an unsatisfying slumber, drawing her attention to something. Something she would already know, had she not shutdown the part of her brain that sought out psychic activity, was invading her mind.

Somehow, Roxana's subconscious mind had switched back on while she slept. Alerting her to where the danger would be coming from. It was not from where she would have expected.

She had dreamt of a plush white bedroom, in a warm country, but instead of the peace that such a comfortable setting usually brings, there was an oppressive presence which casting an invisible shadow over the scene.

The bed which she had imagined laying on was soft, warm and comforting but as she had tried to move, her legs would not, as though nailed to the bed. No amount of struggling or pressure from her free hands could move her pinned limbs.

The dream had been too vivid to be just a dream. She knew only too well that this was someone else's reality her unconscious mind had zeroed in on. Her ability was so different from her 'colleagues'. Whereas they would only link with those that had been deemed targets, she would be drawn into linking with those often needing help and demonstrating a higher than average psychic ability. Although, this was different, whoever was at the other end of the link had no ability whatsoever.

For the first time in what seemed like an eternity, although it had actually only been a few weeks, Roxana put herself into a Mindsweep.

A Mindsweep was a deep, trance like state that others like her would use to seek out threats, information, or people. It was a useful skill, pioneered during the Cold War by the CIA, under the guidance of Dr Marcus Harrison.

Harrison built the Mindsweeper Project on the back of the failed Project Stargate, in which psychics were trained to be remote viewers. Remote viewing had been deemed an unimportant undertaking, yielding disappointing results. It was a perfect cover for expanding Mindsweeper, stepping up its development into an infiltration program.

Roxana had superhuman psychic abilities, coupled with the techniques developed from the original Mindsweeper project, made her a formidable adversary for anyone, and sometimes more so for those with similar skills. For hers would always be superior.

With her eyes closed, she breathed deeply. All conscious thought drifted away, limiting distractions and freeing her mental pathways for the information she would be seeking out. Her mind worked much like a radio, but receiving on all frequencies simultaneously instead of scanning the bandwidth one frequency at a time. She had to filter out so much white noise in order to locate the one signal that was the target. Her mind was a very precise tool. Within a minute she had focused on the mind of a woman in Southern Spain. Any other Mindsweeper may have taken up to an hour to find the target and the subsequent link would have only been very brief.

As Roxana entered the woman's mind, she immediately saw the same white room that had appeared in her dream, this time she was seeing it all from the woman's eyes instead of her own. A glance at the foot of the bed revealed the reason for the immovable legs. Two pair of handcuffs secured the woman's ankles to the heavy cast iron and wooden bed frame. The woman was in trouble.

With a direct link firmly established, she was about to drop out of the trance but sensed something else was wrong.

Deep within the woman's subconscious there was a command thought. A command thought was a platform from which an individual could be programmed to do anything and have no knowledge of whatever the task was. The technique was to place a set of instructions into the mind of the subject whilst they slept, the instructions would then be activated by the Mindsweeper who had place the command or triggered by a random act familiar to the subject. The command thought, called an anchor, once placed was impossible to overcome and difficult to remove.

The anchor that she had found was left by a very skilled Mindsweeper but not by herself or any her colleagues. The process by which a Mindsweeper worked was unique to the individual, much like fingerprints. This anchor had acted as a beacon drawing Roxana to it. She would have to remove it, freeing the woman of its presence. A dormant anchor would often disturb the mental pathways, causing any number of psychological conditions. Leaving it was not an option. Not only would she have to remove it but replace it with something else, something more useful.

---

Nina sat bolt upright on the bed. There was something drifting through her mind, something bizarre yet familiar. She was not having a dream or a nightmare, this was her reality.

The cuffs still bound her to the bed but that was not what had woken her.

The familiar, yet unusual, sensation flowed swiftly into her brain, pressuring the sleepy serotonin out, forcing alertness. Somebody or something was inside her head.

The last time she had experienced these feelings, she had nearly lost her life. The aftermath of that event had roamed the corridors of her mind for months, taking its own sweet time to become part of her normal consciousness. Normal was nothing like it had been before. There were bouts of insomnia, and anxiety on occasion, usually whenever Nina was tired or under pressure, like now.

This time the sensation was somehow different. Not malevolent or intrusive but comfortable; almost friendly.

Suddenly, she became fully alert. Nina could not remember feeling as sharp as she did right at that moment. All anxiety for her situation melted away. Whatever switch had been flicked within her mind, had given her access to all regions of her cognitive thought.

Nina had never felt so alive.

And that was not the only unusual activity happening from within. She heard a voice, not audible, but it was there. It was subtle, like an inner voice speaking softly, but with a different accent, an American accent, with a hint of something else. It said one sentence for now, and that was enough.

*'Don't be afraid, I am Roxana, and I'm here to help.'*

Chained to a strange bed, against her will, but remarkably, Nina no longer felt alone.

# Chapter Nineteen

"What are you talking about?" Ray asked, "What the fuck is an impenetrable?"

Hogarth shifted in his seat. His discomfort was obvious. He clearly did not want to part with any more information.

"An impenetrable is an individual who cannot be read by a Mindsweeper, or anyone using advanced psychic ability or techniques." Hogarth spat the words out reluctantly.

"I'm not *an impenetrable*" Ray stated, "Langston read me -nearly two years ago."

"How do you know that?" Hogarth leaned forward in his seat.

"He knew why I was visiting him before I had even arrived. He was well aware who I was and the questions I had for him." It was Ray's turn to look smug, "So, your logic is completely fucked and you've kidnapped Nina for no reason at all."

The information did not deter Hogarth in any way, shape or form.

"You were not alone when you visited Langston," Hogarth waited for a nod of recognition which never came, "Langston read Nina, not you. If you had discussed the case and the questions then she would know as much as you would – more, because of her relationship to another Mindsweeper."

Hogarth reclined back into the seat again, letting his words sink in for a moment.

Ray tried to remember his time back in that cosy, coastal cottage and the two days of questioning, trying to understand the inner workings of a covert CIA project. The facts were extracted from the broken mind of a man trying to forget the world he had been involved with decades before. A lot had happened since then. There had been a lot of cases. Too much water had flowed under the bridge to be a hundred percent sure of what was said and by whom.

A flash of recollection sparked across Ray's face.

"Langston read a thought directly from my mind. Your theory is flawed!"

"Did you project it? Think it into his brain, so to speak?" Hogarth's face creased to a quizzical expression.

"Yeah! Maybe, what of it? He still was able to read the thought,"

Hogarth smiled the same smug smile as he did before, he could see that Ray did not know enough about the processes of a Mindsweeper's brain.

"Oh, Mr Dean," Hogarth laughed, "You are an impenetrable. Just face it. Roxana will not know that you are looking for her unless you think a thought directly to her and even then she may not hear you. She has guarded her abilities. Shut them down, so not to alert others of her presence."

Ray exchanged confused glances with Barney again but said nothing. He wanted Hogarth to finish the explanation so he could debunk the theory, or at least learn the next move.

"She will not see you coming. Neither will anyone she is hiding with." Hogarth adopted a stern expression as he knew he had Ray beaten now.

"Who is she likely to be hiding with?" Barney asked the question this time.

Reaching into his jacket pocket, Hogarth pulled two photographs and placed them on the desk. One was of a gaunt young man the other was a screen grab from a

CCTV system, showing two figures, one very tall the other petite, on a high street somewhere in the UK.

"The man is called Jamie Delaney, or 'Spook' to his friends, and there aren't many," Hogarth's finger hovered over the picture then switched to the other image, "and this is a freeze frame from a street camera in Croydon less than 36 hours ago.

Ray picked up the photos and studied them before passing them to his colleague.

"Do you believe them to be still in the Croydon area?" Barney asked. His eyes still exploring the screen grab for details.

"We do. Our Mindsweeper sensed some activity yesterday. Less movement means less interaction with others. If they keep moving, then they run the risk of doing something that we might see," Hogarth leaned back into the chair once more, "Roxana does not want to be found and Spook is her only ally."

Ray took the photos back from Barney and placed them into his own jacket pocket, retrieving his car keys at the same time.

"Who is your 'Mindsweeper'?"

"I only know him as Rogue. A very interesting individual to say the least - he loves the destructive nature of his work," there was admiration in the statement.

"And was it this 'Rogue' who told you I was impenetrable?"

"It was,"

"Ok. Get the fuck out of my office so I can start this bullshit job," Ray had heard enough and rose from his chair as he uttered the words.

Hogarth got up and extended a hand but the gesture was not returned.

"Find our girl and yours will be returned to you, unharmed,"

Ray pointed to the door. There was no need to tell Hogarth how unwelcome he had become. The American knew.

"Unharmed better be right, because if so much as hair on her head is harmed I'll be coming after you. And remember you won't see me coming, I'm impenetrable." Ray felt obliged to return some of the vicious smugness.

Hogarth took a step toward the door, not answering the investigator, just pausing to let the younger of the hired muscle open the door for him.

"I bid you, good luck, Mr Dean, but don't take Mr Barnett with you as he can be read like a book and you will be discovered."

Both investigators held their tongues, neither wanted to furnish the man with any reason to engage them further. The sooner Hogarth was gone, the sooner they could get down to business.

They remained in the office, watching the American leave followed by his two bodyguards.

"Are you going now?" Barney asked.

"Yeah," Ray knew he was not in any fit state but hesitation was not a part of any plan, "I'll head to Croydon, it'll take a few hours to get there but I need you to find out as much as you can on that bastard in the meantime."

Barney simply nodded, patting his friend on the shoulder, there were no words of comfort he could offer. The case started right now, but unlike any other work they did, they could not fail.

There was too much at stake.

# Chapter Twenty

Nina lay on the bed. Her body turned to face the balcony window. If she could not be free of her shackles then at least she could stare at freedom, and the harbour view beyond the glass wall of her makeshift cell.

The voice in her head had been quiet for some time now, there was so much more to know but nobody explaining the Who and the Why there was telepathic conversation happening at all. She took some comfort from the experience but not too much considering the predicament of being held against her will with still no clue as to why.

One of her captors had brought in breakfast about an hour previously. Coffee, croissants and fruit would have been her breakfast of choice, and that is exactly what had been placed beside her.

She reached out, taking the final piece of croissant off the plate, swilling it down with the remnants of her tepid coffee.

Either it was a lucky guess or these people had been observing her for a while, although, the thought that the information may have been obtained by psychic means had occurred to her. It mattered not how they knew *but* that they knew, that worried Nina.

The man called Ghost walked into the room. He did knock first but there was no pause for a response from his captive.

"How are you feeling today?" His question seemed pretty normal under the circumstances.

"I'm great! I think I'll go for a walk later, if that's ok?" she said boldly.

"I am afraid that will not be possible," the sarcasm of the statement had clearly been lost on the Eastern European man.

"I didn't think so." she said, shaking her head, "Why are you here?"

"I am leaving for a few days, so I came to say goodbye…" he was interrupted.

"Goodbye then! I'll see myself out after you've gone,"

"You will be safe with my men," he ignored her comment, "you may be released by the time I return."

"Maybe I'll have escaped by then," Nina smiled a wide sarcastic smile. She was surprised by her own bravado but it felt good. Maybe there was a little bit more to the psychic link that Roxana had made. An injection of confidence perhaps, bolstering her situation.

"That will not be possible," his accent was never more apparent. Her attitude seemed to disturb his train of thought, his English suffering because of it. He turned and walked out of the room, not waiting for a reply.

Nina flopped back on to the bed, contemplating her situation. From the other side of the door she heard the main apartment door slam shut. Ghost must have left.

There were no sounds of activity from beyond the room. Usually there was conversation in one language or another, very rarely in English, but this time there was nothing. No television. No music. No sound of any kind.

It was unsettling.

Nina had contemplated taking a nap, reading a book or putting on the television herself but suddenly she had a very different situation to contend with.

The two men left to watch over Nina entered the room. There was no reason for them to be in the room. The one who had brought in the breakfast was middle aged and slightly overweight. He sweated a lot and his body odour was very obvious every time he entered the room.

The other was young, early twenties and very slim. His cheeks were covered in acne but no stubble as though he had not matured enough to grow any facial hair just yet.

Nina was immediately on her guard.

"What do you want?" her voice broke as she asked the question.

The older man smiled but there was comfort in his expression. These two had a separate agenda, over and above their primary instructions.

"We would like to see more of you lady," the older man said, his breathing had become very rapid in anticipation.

"I don't think your boss would want you in here," Nina's own breath became shallower as the panic of her situation was realised.

"He won't know," the younger man answered, licking his lips.

As both men approached the enchained, helpless Nina, there was no doubt of their intentions now as they started to undress themselves.

# Chapter Twenty One

Mile after mile ticked away on the satnav as the high powered Audi weaved from lane to lane. Undertaking or overtaking, it mattered not to Ray, cars were in the way and he needed to find a path through them. The sooner he got to Croydon, the sooner he could start the search for the mysterious Roxana. The journey would just be a blur of road signs and tail lights until he neared his destination. Such was the level of his focus.

The CD in the player restarted for the second time. Ray had no desire to change the disc. He favoured older rock music if he was travelling any kind of distance. Pink Floyd, Led Zeppelin or U2 in their early days, if the mood took him, were the usual choice, but since Nina had come into his life he had widened his musical scope and listened to several of her choices on their trips away. Today's choice was Rudimental. Ray liked the very different styles on each track due to most of the songs featuring very different artists. He was keen on Emilie Sandi's contribution on two songs and those tracks always reminded him of Nina. Not that he needed reminding of her. She was never far from his thoughts, but the events of the last twelve hours or so had prioritised Ray's mind, so much so that he thought of nothing else. He had to get her back home.

There was a buzz of vibration followed by a double beep from the mobile phone thrown onto the passenger seat, alerting Ray of possible new information. A quick glance at the screen showed that an email had come from the office. The M25 was not the place to be reading emails whilst driving, nowhere was really, but four lanes of fast moving traffic needed due attention over any message received.

Up ahead was a service station. Ray felt he needed a coffee, and a stretch of the legs, on top of looking at the info. He hoped there would be some good news in the email. Maybe he could turn around and head back home. Maybe Nina was already waiting for him.

Wishful thinking was no help.

Ray manoeuvred his car to the far side of the service station carpark. The longer walk might wake him up and inspire some plan of action. For now he was running on empty, clueless as to where to start once he arrived at his destination.

With phone in hand, Ray walked the central path of the car park. The email was not good news, just background information on Shriver and the business dealings of SAED.

The email contained one sentence and several attachments from various technology websites and a couple from a conspiracy theory website.

The technology articles covered the many different aspects of SAED, or Shriver Aviation Electronic Development to give the company its full name, and how the company was rapidly expanding through buying other smaller development companies. One company, however, was mentioned more than once.

Roux L'aeronautique was seen as a company that was reinventing the wheel, so to speak, when it came to aircraft innovation. With the creation of the GravEx wing design, the company was looking to do some expanding of its own. Vincent Roux, the CEO and key share holder was in talks with SAED about a possible merger which would make Roux extremely rich and give SAED a vital commodity in modern avionics design. Both would benefit, but it was the opinion of certain experts that Roux was getting the better end of the deal, with a handsome cut in the mass production of his design but still holding the patent. SAED would get unlimited use of the GravEx design, to sell its own brand of aircraft with the new technology and sell wings to the big players in military aircraft technology, but all licences would remain with Roux.

Most of the articles said much the same thing but all had a different spin on the benefits to both companies. However, the conspiracy theory websites had very different opinions on the merger.

A detail that had not been discussed in the tech pages was the fact that Roux was dead. Beaten to death, in a toilet cubicle at Charles De Gaulle airport, by an unknown assailant on the day he was due to fly out to Los Angeles, where the Headquarters of SAED is based. The conspiracy theorists went wild.

Another detail that seemed overlooked by the tech pages was the apparent suicide of the CEO of SAED, James Shriver. Again the conspiracy theorists lapped up this news, pointing the finger at The New World Order or Illuminati, which ever title fitted best into the propaganda. Money might gain privilege, but it can also gain dangerous and powerful enemies.

It was undeniable, both CEOs, dying in suspicious circumstances within days of each other, and on the cusp of the most important merger in the history of both companies, stank of conspiracy. There was no such thing as tragic coincidence when billions of dollars were at stake.

Through all the articles, whether censored or not, whether based on legitimate fact or the paranoid ramblings of a few jilted individuals, Ray could not see one provable fact to bring hope to his quest.

What disturbed him more was the single sentence that accompanied the attachments.

'There is no information on Hogarth at all.'

Ray was not sure how all this fitted in with Nina's kidnapping or how any of the information was going to help with the search for Roxana and her accomplice but it made him realise that this was a far more sinister case than he ever thought he would have to deal with. Who was Hogarth? Was he just a puppet or the one pulling the strings?

# Chapter Twenty Two

She was frozen beyond fear. The two naked and aroused men were now sitting either side of the bed. The older man started to paw at Nina's body, touching her breasts through her thin white t-shirt, and bra, while the younger man undid the cuff from her left ankle.

She smacked away older man's hands as a natural reaction but he retaliated with the back of his hand across her face. She fell back on to the bed stunned and the man took advantage of her prone position, launching his naked, heavy torso onto her body, slobbering on her exposed neck.

The younger man stroked her twitching legs as they fought against the violation. He pushed the body of his older comrade to get access to Nina's trousers, the purpose of which was all too evident.

With every fibre of strength she could muster she resisted. Her struggle against the superior strength of these two immoral fiends was a futile one.

Hands clawed roughly at her body. She closed her eyes tight in a vain effort to shut out the event. Clothes were pulled at and ripped to one side exposing her breasts.

Eyes squeezed tighter.

Muscles tensed.

Resistance waned.

Then nothing. The touching stopped. The clawing ceased. The weight was lifted from her body.

She slowly opened her eyes. Her taut posture unclenched.

She did not understand what she saw. Both men stood at opposite sides of the bed, frozen in place and staring into space.

*'I won't let them hurt you anymore,'* said the voice in her head.

"Roxana?" Nina spoke out loud.

*'I'm here. Get dressed, get out.'* The voice was firm but comforting.

Nina tried to swing herself off the bed but one of her ankles was still cuffed to the bed frame.

*'Sorry,'* the voice was apologetic and as loud as though spoken from within the room.

The younger man bent down and retrieved the keys from the bedroom floor. Nina flinched at his movement, fearing the attack would resume.

*'Don't worry,'* Roxana's delicate unspoken tone soothed Nina's fears.

The man unlocked the cuff from her ankle and then from the bed. He walked over to the older man, who turned around, and cuffed him. The younger man then reached for the other set of discarded cuffs and placed a bracelet on his own wrist. Then, backing up to his partner, he entwined their arms. A swift snap of the other bracelet locked both men together.

*'Get out!'* echoed loud and clear through her mind.

Nina leapt from the bed, pulling her clothes back into place and swiftly put on her shoes. She crept carefully toward the door leading to the lounge. She had no idea what lay beyond.

The door was slightly ajar revealing very little. She eased the door wider and peered into the room. There were various discarded food cartons and beer cans scattered over a large wooden coffee table. There was a sofa and two matching beige chairs, all pointing toward a large wall mounted television which was switched off.

She stepped into the room, convinced that there were no other men in there waiting to do her harm.

The lounge was bigger than she had anticipated. There was a table and chairs positioned in a small kitchen area toward the furthest wall and two other doors before the main entrance to the apartment.

Steadily, she made her way toward the main door, not wishing to disturb any unseen hostage takers secreted in another room.

Slowly, she made her way past one doorway, which she presumed was bathroom, but something caught her eye as she passed the next open door.

Folded neatly over a chair, in what appeared to be another bedroom, was a uniform; a police uniform. The shoulder patch with Policia was clearly visible. On the dresser next to the bed was a holstered automatic pistol, an ID tag and a few Euros.

Her heart sank as she stepped into the room to examine the ID. It belonged to the older of the two men handcuffed in the other room.

If the local police had been corrupted by whoever had taken her captive, then her options of possible action had been slashed. She could trust no one.

She took the money and fled the apartment. She would be on her own, apart from the intermittent appearance of the mysterious voice somewhere from within her fragile mind. Fear would be a constant companion too, until she was a very long way away from this place. For all the comfort of having an unseen psychic assisting her journey, it was not the same as having another person right there to lean on. In reality she was all alone. There was no comfort in that at all.

# Chapter Twenty Three

The coffee had done the job. Ray had perked up a little, not much, but enough to continue the journey. The rest of the drive had been uneventful and trouble free, unlike the rest of his life.

The traffic through the middle of Croydon was slow moving. Every inch of the road had a car crawling painfully toward a destination. Ray scanned the pedestrians, hoping that he might see a 6 foot 7 inch homeless man and a Romanian psychic just wandering the streets. But of course, he did not.

Although the gradual movement on the roads had been tedious, it did allow him to notice a long stay multi storey carpark. He knew the car was no way to search a busy urban area and would attempt his search on foot.

He parked in a dark corner on the top floor of the six storey building. The top was always less crowded, often empty after dark, which would mean fewer cars for an assailant to hide behind. Not that there would be one. Ray always thought on the paranoid side of normal. It had kept him out of trouble so many times in the past. Anticipating danger, no matter how trivial, was always a good trait to have but in his current state of anxiety, he anticipated danger with every decision he took.

His footsteps echoed off the narrow walls, giving him a disturbing feeling that he could be heard by everyone. The deep clacking of his own steps, accompanied him on his descent down the urine stained stairwell. The acrid smell filled his nostrils. It was not an uncommon smell and probably more so on a Sunday after a busy rugby Saturday. Many a beer filled reveller must have taken relief in the stairwell on the early morning stagger home. The state of the amenities were of no concern to Ray, there were much bigger issues at hand.

Armed with the photos that Hogarth had supplied, he took to the streets of Croydon. He had no idea where to start other than he should start somewhere. And while he walked, looking at the multitude of faces that surrounded him on the busy pedestrianised streets, all he could see was Nina. Her chestnut, shoulder length hair; her high cheek bones; her deep blue eyes; every female face morphed into the features of the only person he wanted to find. But wanting wasn't enough. Finding the psychics was a means to an end. And that end couldn't come soon enough.

# Chapter Twenty Four

The hot Mediterranean sun felt almost comforting. Nina basked in its glow for a moment, as she stepped out of the building, getting her bearings and realising that her apartment block was no more than a mile or so away.

She knew Puerto Banus as well as any town in England. She had both lived and worked in the Spanish town, off and on, for years. But as well as she might know it, Nina anticipated that those that seek to harm her would have better local knowledge. Having at least two local police officers on the payroll was a terrifying disadvantage. Who knew how many other agents or henchmen were prowling the streets of this now foreboding place?

Because of the urgency of her escape, Nina did not look for her bag. No bag would mean she was without her credit cards or keys to the apartment. She could gain entry via the security guard but getting there would have to be on foot, as the only money she had was the few Euros taken from a bedside table back in the place of her captivity, and it wasn't enough for a taxi.

She had to make the decision between the faster, direct route through the centre of the town, where the far reaching tendrils of the organisation that had captured her, might have access to the local CCTV systems and be able to locate her quickly, or she could use the less well travelled back roads and alleys, which may provide her with some degree of concealment, but leave her vulnerable to local hoodlums and criminals that inhabited such places.

With no help from Roxana, Nina chose to take the safer, more direct route and took the gambit on being discovered.

As quickly as she could, without running, Nina paced the long public streets of her second home. The paths had been trodden by her many times, sometimes with Ray, but this time there was none of the calm that she usually felt. Instead, the hot breath of an unseen foe could be sensed on her neck, as the magnitude of her situation hit hard. She was under threat and a very long way from safety.

# Chapter Twenty Five

After many hours and several miles of walking the streets of Croydon, Ray stopped to recharge his exhausted physical and emotional batteries.

He perched himself at an elevated window seat of a busy McDonald's, a coffee and a burger in front of him. He had no desire for either but his body was telling him he needed to stop and recuperate. His limbs felt heavy, his head felt light, but no sleep for thirty six hours and very little food would do that.

As he sipped at the bitter drink through the plastic lid, he reflected on all the places he had been that day and all the people he had talked to. It was as though the locals thought he was crazy. In this day and age nobody walked the streets asking the public if they had seen a missing person but Ray was helpless. He had been forced into a desperate corner with few options.

For the most part, people just ignored him or swiftly shook their heads as they failed to look at the photos. Some even told him to 'Fuck off!' which was more effort than just saying 'no' but they did it anyway.

His phone remained silent throughout. No messages, calls or emails. No news that the situation had changed. No word from either of his colleagues or the man that had forced Ray to work. They say that 'no news is good news' but it really didn't seem that way.

He took a bite from the limp, warm burger, immediately pulling the gherkin from his mouth and dropping it into the cardboard carton. He could only imagine what his expression looked like as he heard a gang of teenagers giggling from the booth on his right. He stared at his reflection in the slightly smudged window, to see what was so amusing, but all he saw was his sad tired face looking back. There was nothing to see. And that was how useful he felt. He felt like nothing. No good to anyone. No good to Nina.

He placed the half eaten burger into the carton, on top of the discarded gherkin, and reached for his coffee. Maybe a further hit of caffeine would jolt his exhausted soul into functioning properly once more. A kick start toward the man he needed to be right now.

But before he could raise the vessel to his lips, he caught sight of a figure on the opposite side of the road.

Dressed head to foot in shabby black clothing, with a hood covering his face, was an exceptionally tall man. He was skinny, walked with an awkward striding gait and carrying a rucksack over one shoulder.

Maybe good fortune would be had today.

# Chapter Twenty Six

He abandoned his food and rushed for the door.

The tall man had almost made the corner of the block by the time Ray made it out onto the pavement.

There was less than a hundred feet of pedestrian filled air between Ray and his quarry, but it could have been a hundred miles as the adrenaline filled his heavy legs, making them heavier still and the pursuit that much more difficult. Ray tried to sprint but an awkward faltering run was as much as he could manage. The tall man was now out of view.

The pedestrianised road was filled with shoppers and commuters going about their business, blocking Ray from doing his. He barged passed one man who yelled at him for his discourtesy but Ray was too focused on trying to see where the tall man had disappeared to. This was a high speed race, and Ray was running in slow motion.

He made the corner but had to stop and stare at the sea of bobbing heads before him. Just when he thought that he had found one of his targets, he bore a sense of colossal disappointment that the target was lost already.

Maybe tiredness and the need to find these people had played tricks with his mind, that an apparition had been created by his exhausted consciousness to ease his painful soul.

Just as he stopped with a desperately heavy heart, he caught sight of a hooded head rise out of the crowds, just a few inches, but enough to alert Ray that he had not imagined the man at all.

With renewed vigour, he dodged and weaved through the bustling throng, keeping his eyes on the target. This time he would not lose the tall man. This time he would keep up.

He fought against the tide of bodies, just as he thought progress was being made, a slow moving pedestrian would block the way. Two steps forward, one step back - the story of Ray's life.

He inched ever closer to the man who was oblivious to the pursuit. But Ray made a mistake.

As the tall man was about to turn another corner, Ray's mouth didn't utter a word, but his subconscious yelled '*STOP!*'

The tall man stopped dead in his tracks, his head tilted like a confused dog, turning back to look over his shoulder. Ray's plea had been mentally projected for the psychic to hear loud and clear.

As their gazes met, Ray realised he was looking directly into the frightened, wide eyes of Jamie Delaney. He had found Spook.

Spook turned and ran as fast as his legs could carry him, he for one, was not worried about who he knocked down in his attempt to escape from his pursuer.

Desperate times required desperate measures. The road was no longer pedestrianised, so Ray hopped the barrier, and sprinted along the gap between it and the traffic. With no lumbering bodies to block his way, he gained on his target.

Spook afforded another glance over his shoulder.

Ray caught the panicked expression of a man who did not want to be caught and the desperation at how much ground Ray was gaining.

"DELANEY!" Ray shouted as he ran, "STOP!"

The tall, awkward creature ducked down the first alley he came to in an attempt to elude Ray.

Ray hopped back over the barrier and followed.

Spook stood rigid in the centre of the alley, panting for his life. The escape route had led nowhere. It was a dead end.

The tall figure slowly turned toward Ray. There was so much fear in those deep, dark eyes of this lost creature. Ray pitied him.

"I'm not here to hurt you," he spoke with a calm voice, "I just need to find Roxana,"

Spook could barely breathe to answer, he was panting so hard.

Ray was patient enough to allow the young man to compose himself.

"I need your help Jamie," again, he used a soothing tone, "please help me find Roxana,"

"Spook!" the man spat out between rapid breaths.

"What?" Ray puzzled.

"Nobody calls me Jamie," the trembling air of panic was apparent in his voice "they always call me Spook."

"Ok, Spook, please help me."

"Who are you?" Spook asked tilting his head again.

"My name is Ray Dean. I'm a private investigator and I've been hired to find Roxana Petrescu."

There was no immediate response from the perplexed man backed into the alley. Spook's head pitched and tilted but at no time did he take his eyes from his pursuer.

"What's troubling you?" Ray asked.

"I can't read you," Spook said it as if Ray should understand what he was talking about.

"No, you won't be able to," the word impenetrable flashed across his mind but he did not want to say it out loud.

"I don't know if you are telling me the truth,"

Ray understood but couldn't really comprehend the young man's dilemma.

For his whole life, Spook had been able to read what was true, and what was deception, the psychic gift was taken for granted, but now he would have to trust without the use of his power.

"You're going to have to trust me," Ray edged closer to the shabby young man, "I do not wish to harm you or Roxana. I just need your help."

"Angel!" Spook uttered quietly.

"I beg your pardon?"

"I call her, Angel," Spook looked for answers in the eyes of the man who scared him. Scared him more than any other man he had ever met before, except for Rogue. Spook would always fear Rogue.

"OK! Please, take me to Angel," the name felt wrong but Ray wasn't going to argue.

Without another word, he followed the psychic from the alleyway and hopefully toward his objective; although he took nothing for granted. How could he?

# Chapter Twenty Seven

The air conditioning in the taxi was just not up to the Mediterranean heat. Ghost stepped out of the cab after what seemed like an endless trip to Malaga Airport.

Grabbing his bag, he handed over a wad of Euros to the driver. He didn't need to count it knowing it was more than enough for the trip. He smiled as he read the driver's mind over the very generous tip.

Dropping his bag to the pavement, he pulled out his cigarettes. The pack was almost crushed but there was at least one smoke-able cigarette. He screwed the slightly bent smoke into the corner of his mouth and lit it.

As he enjoyed his first hit of nicotine of that day his phone rang.

"Hello," he knew who it was without looking at the display.

"Put out your cigarette and get back to the apartment," the voice said sternly.

"There is no time, my flight boards in an hour."

"Roxana helped the girl to escape. We need the Fuller woman back at the apartment,"

Ghost opened his mind, swiftly trying to connect to the men back at the apartment but he could not link to either of the police henchmen he had left guarding Nina. It was likely that Roxana had entered their minds, aided in Nina's escape and then fixed a blocking thought in the minds of both men. He would have to remove any interfering thoughts once he got back to his men but knew that he was not skilled enough to keep the superior Mindsweeper out of their heads indefinitely.

"What has happened?" Ghost asked. If he had missed something obvious the repercussions would be immense.

"Those two idiots decided to have their fun but didn't bank on Roxana stepping in. Fuller is on the run and we need her back to make Dean work our way," the voice at the other end of the line increased in volume.

"I don't understand. I couldn't sense it." Ghost grew confused by the failure of his ability.

"Of course you couldn't sense it, she's better than you. She's probably with Spook and she can do anything she wants to now. Get back and fix this now." The line went dead.

He knew that there was no point in arguing. It was his fault that the girl had escaped and he was going to pay for it, one way or another. He might have been a very powerful Mindsweeper on the outside, but he was still just a lost Polish boy on the inside. He was raised to be a killer but it had never been what he wanted. Ghost was a puppet, a puppet for those that gave him the creature comforts; a bribed life, for unlimited use of his gift. And while others were superior, he was still formidable.

He drew a lungful of smoke and flicked the half smoked cigarette into the road. With a raised arm, a taxi quickly pulled up in the empty bay. He got in.

If Roxana and Spook were now together then the game had changed considerably. As a unit they were invincible.

The advantage had to be regained, at all costs. And that would mean someone would have to pay dearly. Ghost prayed it wouldn't be him.

He also feared that Rogue may take charge.

Rogue didn't do sympathy or empathy. Rogue didn't do anything that was pleasant or amiable.

Rogue did malicious. Even on a good day.

# Chapter Twenty Eight

Rogue – One Year Earlier

The wait was a ponderous one. He sat in the passenger seat of a SAED SUV, with a tutting driver sat next to him. Rogue only ever addressed his chauffeur as 'Driver', not because he didn't know his name but because he didn't wish to associate with a mere minion of the company.

In truth, Rogue knew everything about the large muscular man assigned to drive for him. He knew his name was Kyle Simpson. He knew the man was cheating on his wife with an aerobics teacher fifteen years his junior. He knew the man had three children, two with his wife and one by his childhood sweetheart who he never talks to or about, because he had been too young to be laden with a child at eighteen years old.

Rogue knew every little dark secret the man had. Not through conversation or idle gossip, but from the gift he wielded recklessly. He had intruded on the driver's mind many times and took relish in living the most intimate moments of the man's life.

As they continued to wait, he subtly drifted into the driver's mind once more, he could see the thoughts as though played on a giant TV screen, still conscious of everything else that was happening but occasionally glancing at the imaginary screen to the see what his driver was accessing from memory.

The man was currently thinking of his lover's body and how much more desirable it was than his wife's. The firmness of her thighs as she sat astride him, the flex of her taut abdomen as she grinded on him during a surreptitious liaison, the aesthetically perfect figure of a woman in prime condition, as she walked around a motel room, naked. Rogue enjoyed the man's thoughts, it thrilled him.

Suddenly there was movement from the house they had parked opposite.

"Stop daydreaming of your bendy lady friend and stay focused." Rogue didn't care whether the man knew he had been inside his mind.

The driver just shot a disgusted look at the psychic and started the engine.

\*

Gil Peters stepped out of his large LA townhouse, as he did every weekday morning. He popped the locks on his Chrysler Voyager, opened the passenger door and dropped his briefcase onto the seat. He slammed it shut and then opened the rear passenger door.

This morning would be slightly different. His wife was out of town for a business meeting, he would have to run his two daughters to school.

"Gabby! Ana! The car's open," Gil called to his children.

Nine year old Gabriella and six year Anastasia trotted out of the house, sporting matching red and white gingham dresses, matching Disney Princess backpacks, complete with lunchboxes and drinks bottles. Their long blonde hair was tied into plaits, using matching ribbon. The only significant difference between the girls, other than their age and height, was that Ana carried an 'Anna' soft toy doll wherever she went. She and the character, from her favourite film Frozen, shared a name so it was only fitting that she had the toy.

The girls clambered into the back of the Voyager, toy Anna was placed in the centre seat, as the girls took their places on their matching booster seats.

Gil locked the house and made his way back to the car to strap his daughters in safely. He didn't notice the black SUV parked, engine running, on the other side of the road. Why would he?

It was a typical Monday morning. He would make his way to the SAED building, albeit via school, and sit down to the usual round of board meetings on how to expand the company. Although, the company was named after Shriver, the major shareholder with thirty-five percent of the share value, Gil was number two with twenty percent. For some time now, Shriver had been trying to buy Gil Peters out of that twenty percent. With a stake of fifty-five percent, Shriver would have the controlling share value, giving him full control of the entire company.

Gil did not want to sell his share, not just yet anyway.

The dark blue Voyager pulled out of the drive and headed toward the freeway.

The SAED SUV followed at a safe distance.

Instead of the usual news only KNX radio station, Gil had been coerced into playing Disney movie music. The girls laughed and sang badly, and often out of tune, to all their favourites. Even when the dark threatening clouds released their liquid payload onto the busy Los Angeles streets, the atmosphere inside the vehicle couldn't be dampened.

The rain hammered down on the roof but it couldn't be heard over the volume of the music system. There was no sun shining down on Sunset Boulevard, and the regularly placed palm trees that adorned the sidewalk looked less than tropical, but the joy that emanated from the backseat cut through the gloom outside. At every red light other commuters turned their heads and couldn't help but feel the merriment.

It was a wonderful sight on a miserable day. But things can change so quickly.

*

The driver peered through the windscreen, trying to see the Voyager between the wipers as they swooped back and forth at the highest setting.

Rogue didn't need his eyes to see anything. His mind saw it all. He could see the road ahead and the flow of traffic. He could see the traffic lights and how they would halt vehicles at the bigger intersections. He could also see all the approaching traffic that would converge on the big four lane intersection just a couple of miles ahead.

What he was looking for, he eventually found.

A large semi-truck, with a trailer, travelling parallel on Hollywood Boulevard and the driver was tired.

Rogue closed his eyes, merging his mind with that of the semi-truck driver. It was easy for him to do. The years of experimentation, fine tuning and repetition made it second nature.

There was no need to explore the man's mind, just take control turning the vehicle of his profession in to deadly weapon. The Mack Pinnacle truck would go from being the work engine of the American truck driver, to fourteen thousand pounds of catastrophic killing machine in an instant.

And that instant would be at Rogue's discretion.

He tried to accelerate the vehicle but the heavy payload made it difficult. Rogue swerved the truck across from the far left lane into a diagonal spanning all three lanes, nudging cars as it did so. Then the truck halted, blocking all lanes.

Rogue made the driver hop out of the cab after applying the independent brakes of both the trailer and the truck. He took a heavy wrench that was loose in the foot-well, just in case anyone took issue with the position of the trailer.

Horns blasted and angry commuters yelled at the truck driver but he heard nothing. The truck driver would only know the gravity of what was happening after his mind was returned to him.

As the driver was releasing the air-lines and the electrical hook-up, an irate commodities broker, who had strayed from his BMW, decided to see *'What the hell was going on?'*

The question was answered by a greasy wrench to the side of the head. The broker dropped to the tarmac, skull fractured; unconscious, but alive.

Without lowering the trailer supports, the driver released the gripping jaws of the fifth wheel. This detached the trailer making the truck quicker and able to use all 500 brake horse power to get up to top speed. Eight metric tons of metal at eighty miles per hour, made the truck deadlier than any bullet. At least with a bullet, there would be a chance of survival.

Rogue controlled the driver back into the cab and he accelerated away. The trailer was dragged a few feet before it crashed onto the freeway, blocking all the frustrated commuter traffic behind.

The timing had to be precise. In his minds eyes, Rogue could see the view from the cab using the vision of the driver. He could also see the position of both the truck and Voyager from a remote viewer's aerial perception. All of the psychics learned to remote view before they learned to Mindsweep. To them it was like learning to walk before they could run.

The Voyager would hit the intersection as the lights were green and pull straight out.

The blockade causes by the trailer allowed the truck a virtually clear road right up to the same intersection. It didn't matter that the lights would be red.

Rogue simply thought 'faster' and the truck driver forced the speeding vehicle up through the gears. As the speed increased, the momentum intensified. Lethality grew by the second.

The truck was aimed between the only two cars at the halt line. It cleaved through them like a child's oversized toy hurled through a line of dominos. The insignificant vehicles offered little resistance, crumpling like tin cans.

The target was in sight but oblivious to everything, except for the vehicle directly in front and the joyous singing from behind.

Rogue was not one to exclude a subject from the full horror of what was about to unfold.

He released the mind of the truck driver seconds before impact. Enough time to acknowledge what was happening but not enough to take any evasive action; the driver would always think he had fallen asleep at the wheel, never knowing the truth.

\*

Rogue's eyes flickered open. He immediately nudged his driver's shoulder and pointed at the road ahead.

"Watch!" the relish of evil pride crested his tongue.

The carnage took but a few seconds.

The truck impacted the dark blue Voyager at the driver's side door, ploughing through the smaller vehicle, instantly pulverising it. Fragments of metal, plastic and glass were scattered across the intersection. There was very little left to indicate a car, just a shattered pile of broken components and the greasy stench of diesel. It was swift and brutal.

The deep screech of rubber against wet tarmac followed as the guilty vehicle thundered to a halt. Once the truck had stopped moving, there was a silence; a stunned stillness. The only sound was that of the rain pounding against the metal of the immovable morning traffic, as though people couldn't breathe - taking a breath would make the event real.

The horror of a smashed car, twisted metal panels and a contorted steel chassis, adorned in ripped material and miniscule fragments of cubed glass; if devastation was an art form, this was a masterpiece. Only the buckled wheels gave an indication of what the broken structure had been.

What seemed like minutes, was actually only seconds. As the world started to inhale again, the exhaled screams of traumatised witnesses filled the air.

Amongst the splintered pieces of vehicle, strewn across the dark, wet road, was a sodden and blood splattered Anna doll; a beloved toy, never to be held by a child again. Only to be held in desolate sorrow by a wife and mother at a funeral, where three odd sized caskets would be surrounded by a mass of black clothed mourners, a week after this cataclysmic event.

Rogue's driver broke from his speechless state.

"Why?" the disgust almost choked him. A tear for the thought of his own daughters trickled down the cheek of the hardened man, "Why not wait until he had dropped them off?"

Rogue looked at his chauffeur.

"Where would the fun in that be?" a wry smile without a single ounce of remorse accompanied the comment.

Those were the last words exchange by the pair that day.

# Chapter Twenty Nine

Roxana perched herself at the edge of the bed. She wasn't sure whether she should run and hide or stay and face the music. Spook had been compromised, she already knew it, and it was Ray Dean who had found him.

Sooner or later there would be nowhere else for her to run. What would she do then? The world was ever shrinking with only so many places left for her to hide. Eventually, her luck had to run out but maybe this wouldn't be bad luck. Maybe it was supposed to be this way.

Only when the internet and the conspiracy theorist went crazy at the discovery of psychic assassins, trained by the CIA and killing their own, had Roxana taken any interest to read all the articles. She knew all about Ray Dean and how he had been badged as a charlatan by some sites and a hero by others. She could not penetrate his mind, and because of this, she feared him.

It was no coincidence that the captive woman, held by her so called colleagues in Spain, happened to be the life partner of Ray Dean.

Whilst inside the mind of Nina Fuller, Roxana had learned many things. She had learned that Nina was successful, that she had been subject to an intrusive psychic attack before and that her partner, Ray Dean, was a good man who could be trusted.

Maybe this was the man that could help her. Maybe he could offer her a solution or give her a place to hide. It was difficult to trust others when you can look deep into the very core of their minds and see the all the cogs turning; seeing all the agendas and the secrets. Most people were an open book to her but not Ray.

Roxana had to make a decision. Was this the man she could trust with her life? It would be a whole new experience for her if he was.

Getting to her feet, she reached up, grasping at thin air, stretching her back and arms after a brief nap. Her mind was tired. Having to link with Nina over such a distance was draining but she would have to forge that link again, shortly. Roxana knew it was only a matter of time before the escape was reported back to the powers that be. Nina would need her help again.

As she stepped toward the window, her mind drifted into a link with Spook. It was effortless, as their minds had been almost as one for so long.

She could see the passenger side of a dashboard. Spook's head was down, as it usually was. She willed him to lift his eyes and look around.

The street that she viewed from the young man's eyes was just a mile or so away. Spook turned his head, changing the view to a profile view of the driver.

Ray Dean had both hands on the wheel, as though he needed to grip with both for fear of losing control. Anxious lines were etched into his face, as weary eyes scanned the road ahead. Roxana wanted to put this man's mind at ease, for he could only help her if he was performing at his best. She had seen, first-hand, the work that her pursuers were capable of. Even with the aid of a Mindsweeper, or two, Ray would have to be far beyond the best that he could be.

She watched, remotely from the passenger seat, as Ray turned his head toward the scruffy young man sitting next to him. She saw the flicker of recognition in his eyes. He knew he was being viewed by a different Mindsweeper. Maybe he was as good as they said he was. His eyes turned back to the road ahead and Roxana severed the link with Spook.

Within the next few minutes or so, either her saviour or her downfall, would pull up outside. How much would she tell him? How much could she trust him with? Her hand fell to the small swelling in her abdomen. She stroked it, protecting it. Would she tell Ray Dean of her secret? Maybe she wouldn't have to, but this was not how she pictured her life as she progressed toward motherhood. Where did it all go wrong?

# Chapter Thirty

The bustling streets of Puerto Banus appeared not to care about her predicament. Nina had to keep starting and stopping, dodging and weaving. Sometimes, just putting one foot in front of the other was a difficulty.

Too many people lined the pavements, making a speedy return to the apartment no longer a possibility. She would have run on the roads if it wasn't for the many super cars that raced around the streets. She also needed to keep her profile as low as possible. Running would have drawn too much attention. The only people running in Puerto Banus were on treadmills in air conditioned gyms. It wasn't an option.

With every step taken she sensed eyes looking at her. Were they friend or were they foe? She couldn't tell. Until she was at the relative safety of her apartment, she would treat everyone as foe. In these circumstances paranoia was an advantage.

As she stepped onto the marina, Nina was hit by an overwhelming sense of déjà vu. There was a sensation drifting around in the core of her consciousness, trying to gain a foothold. It was familiar, disturbing like a reoccurring violation. It was not the same sensation she felt when Roxana entered her mind. This was very different.

As the crowds thinned out she decided to make a break and run for it. Hopefully this time there wouldn't be somebody waiting to pounce armed with a Taser. At least it was daytime and that might be her ally.

Her arms pumped as she sprinted along the tarmacked marina path. The soft canvas shoes were far from the best thing to be running in, knowing she would pay for it later, but for now Nina just wanted to get to somewhere safe and stop looking over her shoulder, even for just a minute.

As she rounded the corner at the end of the marina, an image flashed across her mind so vividly, she stopped running. It flashed again. It was the view from the backseat of a car. She forced her eyes shut to see the image again but it was not there. Whatever it was, it meant something and she did not like it one bit.

She resumed running but at a gentler pace. If she ran into any undesirables she wanted plenty in reserve if she needed to run for her life.

Upon entering the road on which her apartment was situated, Nina could see there were no assailants waiting to capture her. It was a relief but of no comfort just yet. She longed to be in sight of her Bristol apartment; back with Ray, where everything made sense.

In her head it was simple, get in, get changed, get some money, get her passport and get out of town. A swift shower would be in order too. It hadn't escaped her notice that 36 hours cuffed to a bed in a stressful situation had left her feeling grimy and uncomfortable.

She mounted the stairs to her apartment block just as a searing pain hit her straight between the eyes; as though a diamond had exploded in her brain, shards ripping through the soft delicate membranes within her skull. She dropped like a stone onto the wide white marble steps. She couldn't see the steps or the building. Her eyes were seeing the view from the backseat of a car again. This time it lasted for a few seconds. She could see it was a taxi; a Spanish taxi. The road was very familiar. The main highway between Malaga airport and Puerto Banus, she knew it well.

Then the image was gone. Nina picked herself up and touched her forehead, making sure that the pain had not left a wound of some kind. She did not understand how but she knew exactly what was happening.

\*

Ghost breathed deeply. His eyes were closed and his mind was clear but no matter how hard he tried, he could not link with Nina Fuller's mind. Either she was dead or worse, had help.

The taxi was a good twenty minutes out from Puerto Banus and she already had a head start. It was far from ideal.

He reached for his phone and punched into his contacts ROGUE.

"Are you calling for help?" the voice from the other end of line said.

"You already know I am," Ghost replied in fearful resignation.

"It's already on its way," The line went dead. No goodbye or told you so.

Ghost dropped the phone onto the seat. Nina had help, he knew it. Not physical help but psychic help, either Spook or Roxana, or possibly both. This was not going to end well. The last thing he had wanted to do was ask for the help of Rogue to clear up the mess.

*

Nina made it into her room with a spare key from the building warden. It felt good to be in familiar surroundings but it still didn't feel safe. A lock, a chain, and five centimetres of fireproof wood, were not going to stop the kind of people that used psychics as assassins.

She kicked off her shoes, passing a cursory eye over the red marks on her feet left by the unforgiving material. Just as she stepped into the bathroom to flick on the shower, a message came in loud and clear. Not on a phone or laptop but directly into her brain. Two words from Roxana that made Nina catch her breath.

*'Ray's here,'*

It was what she needed to hear, for now.

# Chapter Thirty One

The deep pile carpet and creaking panel board beneath, making the corridor floor seem spongy. Ray had been in many budget hotels, this was the same as all the others; matching décor, matching carpet, matching doors. Been in one, been in them all.

He followed Spook through the hotel. The scent of unwashed clothing and stale body odour swirled in his nostrils. Ray mentally suggested a shower and a change of clothes but Spook did not hear it.

The psychic stopped at the very last door at the end of the corridor. Ray watched as the awkward young man searched for the key card. He also noticed that the room was the closest to the fire exit, it made excellent sense, the pair of fugitives had obviously thought about an escape plan. It was the details that made Ray not underestimate them.

After poking a finger in to every pocket, Spook eventually pulled the card from his back pocket and tapped it against the door panel. The door clicked and they entered room.

Ray wasn't sure what to expect. He did not think that Roxana would be sitting casually at the edge of one of the single beds as she was. The photo Ray had been shown did not do her justice. Long jet black hair spiralling to just below her shoulders, dark olive complexion with huge black eyes set perfectly on her exquisite face. She was a beauty, but deadly with it.

"Roxana?" Ray asked even though he had no doubt.

"Angel!" Spook corrected.

"Yes, you may call me Roxana but Jamie prefers to call me Angel," her accent was ninety-nine percent American, with just a teasing hint of her Romanian heritage in a slightly husky voice. It was the voice of a woman who had lived a life, a voice befitting of someone much more mature.

"Whatever," Ray was in no mood to play name games, "who are these people that are looking for you?"

"My, I mean," she corrected herself whilst gesturing toward Spook, "our former employers, I would imagine."

"Employers! What were you employed to do?" Ray couldn't disguise his frustration, "Do you kidnap people too?"

"No. And by the way, Nina has escaped. For now,"

The words hit hard. Ray's heart spiked instantly, he could feel the heat of his racing blood flowing through his veins, mixing with adrenaline. The comment interrupted the train of thought in his already chaotic mind.

"What do you mean? How do you know? WHO ARE YOU PEOPLE?" The anger poured from the private detective's mouth.

"Please stay calm Ray," her voice was still calm, even while talking to a very agitated man, "I helped Nina to escape. She's at her apartment, for now, but they will try to capture her again."

"WHAT IS GOING ON? WHO ARE 'THEY'?" Ray smashed his fist onto the counter top of the dressing table. The unused tea cups bounced and rattled in their saucers under the force of the blow.

"This is not helping you, us, or Nina. You need to calm yourself now, and I will tell you the whole story." she said, remaining neutral.

Ray took a moment, breathing deeply before taking a seat in the corner of the room.

"I'm all ears," It was the first time Ray hadn't asked a question since walking into the room.

Roxana patted the end of the bed next to her for Spook to sit down. It was obvious she was more concerned by the mental state of the young homeless man than she was for the mental state of the investigator.

Spook sat beside her but his eyes never left Ray.

With an arm wrapped around him like a mother comforting an injured child, she addressed Spook first.

"It's OK Jamie, he's upset like we are but he's going to help us." Her eyes flicked toward Ray hoping that her statement was a truthful one.

"I can't read him." Spook uttered.

"I know Jamie, I know. I can't read him either but I know he's a good man and he will help us." Her eyes now stared at the unknown factor perched on the chair, "Won't you?"

"Tell me what I need to know, help me get Nina back and I will do everything and anything," he was sincere.

"What do you want to know first?"

"Who is going to re-capture Nina?" Ray directed the question only at Roxana.

"Ghost."

"Ghost?" Ray spat, "Do you all have titles?"

"You already know that we are Spook and Angel but there is also Ghost," Roxana looked vulnerable for the first time, like the words were painful to speak.

"And who is this Ghost? Is he like you? Is he a Mindsweeper too?"

"He is," Roxana swallowed hard, "he is a Mindsweeper. His real name is Jakub Bartek."

Ray pulled out his phone and punched into his contacts. He asked Roxana to spell the name out and gave the information directly to Pete. The whole exchange took only a few seconds. He hung up and dropped his phone on the floor in front of him.

"What is Ghost like?" Ray asked.

"He is a good man but he is loyal to our employers and will do all that he is asked to do," Roxana said.

"Will he hurt her?"

"Not unless he's asked to do so,"

There was no comfort in the answer.

"Is there anyone else I should know about? Is there a 'Maverick' and 'Goose' too?" The sarcasm was lost on the couple.

"No, but there is Rogue," her eyes dropped to the floor.

Ray could sense more than just fear in her voice.

"Is Rogue a good man or a bad man?"

Spook shuffled uncomfortably next to Roxana.

"He's evil," this time Spook piped up.

"And what is his name?" Ray asked.

The time from the question being asked, to the answer being given, seemed like an eternity. Roxana's chest heaved as though the words were impossible to say out loud. Ray could not possibly fathom the depth of the answer.

"His name is Miguel Sanchez," Tears cascading her flawless cheeks.

Ray's mind flipped over several times trying to process the information. Surely it was just a common surname and not the obvious parallel that presented itself at the forefront of his thinking.

But Roxana knew what Ray was thinking. She could not read his thoughts like she could with others, but she could see where his mind had taken him and he was not wrong.

"Yes, it is Manny Sanchez' son."

It was a sucker punch to his very core. Ray could barely breathe. The information winded him, immobilised him with dread. Fear was all that inhabited his being. Surely this day couldn't get any worse. But knowing Ray's luck, possibly.

# Chapter Thirty Two

When the taxi arrived back at his apartment complex, Ghost was surprised to see his two disgraced henchmen sitting on the bonnet of a car. The first thought to enter his head was, *'Why are they not out searching?'*

The taxi stopped next to the car. Ghost passed a large denomination note to the driver and got out, again not waiting for the change.

"I told you not to touch her. I know English is not your first language BUT you do understand it, do you not?"

The two corrupt cops remained silent; their shame too obvious to deny.

"Also, why are you not out looking for her?" Ghost demanded.

"Rogue called, he said to wait here for you," the older cop spoke.

"What about Fuller?"

"She is back at her apartment, there is already a team waiting for her if she should leave,"

Without another word Ghost got into the back of their car.

The younger cop spoke to his colleague in their native Spanish as they entered the car. The older cop clearly replied in agreement but said nothing more.

"Just because I do not speak your language do not think that I cannot read your thoughts." Ghost slapped his hand on the young cops shoulder, "You fucked up, you let her escape and do not think that Rogue will have forgotten that."

Rogue never forgot anything. He always made people pay for their mistakes, even if the punishment didn't fit the crime, they would always pay, dearly; sometimes with their life, or worse, with their mind.

# Chapter Thirty Three

Ray put down his phone for the second time since entering the room. He had made a second call to Pete and filled him in on all the new information. In his haste, he had forgotten to say that Nina had escaped and was back at the apartment. Not that it would have done any good, anyone who could have helped was at least a two hour flight away; Nina would have to fend for herself for now.

He also *had* to pass on the information about the son of Manny Sanchez being one of the Mindsweepers. Rogue's father had been so skilled, he had managed to transcend death and live within the mind of one of the Cold War Mindsweepers, Edward Langston, for more than thirty years. Only time would tell if it was a case of 'like father, like son'.

Ray took out a recording device and placed it on the dressing table counter.

"Please tell me all you can about your *employers*." Ray directed the question at the female psychic.

"How far back do you want me to go?" Roxana asked.

"As far as you need to." Ray wanted to know her entire story. One so young, yet so powerful, must have a tale to tell.

Roxana first spoke about her childhood. She could barely remember her early years but she could recall leaving the orphanage and being taken to a small facility for gifted children. Although she could not remember her first meeting with him, she said that Rogue was already living at the facility, as he was under the care of the institute's founder, Dr Marcus Harrison.

Harrison was the original research scientist of Project Mindsweeper and the person who created the training programs for all the psychics to expand their abilities.

Not known as Rogue back then, just plain Miguel, he was the oldest child of about a dozen gifted individuals, often bullying the others. Not like a school bully, with beatings or intimidation, but by using the gift he was born with; the gift he had inherited from his father.

Like his father before him, Miguel would intrude into the subject's mind while they slept. Instead of taking control of their bodies, he would create nightmares, disturbing the child who was the subject of the attack.

Roxana was the subject of many such attacks; although Miguel hadn't figured on the youngest psychic being more powerful than him. He was already troubled that 'a girl' had similar abilities as him, but when she was able to counter the nightmares, even while she remained asleep, it displeased him, intensely.

It was apparent that Roxana's arrival had caused a major stir at the facility, being the first orphan to be brought the Iron Curtain. The now defunct, Soviet Union, had a very successful remote viewer program and developed many psychics for the purpose of spying. It was because of the Soviet effort in this field that the CIA had to have an adequate response, giving rise to an American made remote viewer program called Project Stargate.

From Project Stargate came Project Mindsweeper and the whole saga of psychics being used as assassins began.

With the Berlin Wall coming down in the autumn of 1989, there was a greater freedom of movement from the former Soviet states. Not only migration from East to West but also more visitors from the West with the money and resources to seek out gifted orphans to offer them a better life. Or so the story goes.

Roxana wasn't the only Eastern European child to arrive at the facility in the years that followed the collapse of the wall. A handful of children of varying ages came and went but only one other, a Polish lad, stayed and developed with the rest. That lad was Jakub Bartek.

Jakub and Roxana were of a similar age and because of their shared Eastern Blok heritage, they formed a very strong bond, so much so that Roxana was able to protect Jakub from the nocturnal attacks instigated by the troubled son of Manny Sanchez.

After a few years of schooling, in both general education and the ways of psychic development there were only Roxana, Jakub and Miguel left. All three had tremendously powerful abilities, but Roxana stood out. She could switch off her ability at will. Also she wasn't confined to using her power over a restricted distance either. The power that she wielded made her the perfect psychic weapon but she resisted, not wanting to be used as such.

On Roxana's tenth birthday, Harrison introduced a new child to the group, that child was Jamie Delaney. Jamie was a psychic phenomenon who could stay in state for an indefinite amount of time. When the others had been exhausted, he could continue. This was also his curse. Jamie would often wake in a psychic trance, making him vulnerable to Miguel's particular form of torture. So much so, that Jamie rarely slept, giving him his distinct gaunt look. With the look, came the nickname. Spook had been born.

Over ten years, as the children turned into adults, they were given every advantage that only the wealthiest of American children had. They attended the best schools, took the best vacations and were truly privileged, at least, the part of their upbringing that was on show. Behind the scenes, the four psychics were groomed and developed to have very different aspirations in life.

With no more cold war, and modern technology at a level that rendered psychic spying for military purposes almost obsolete, their talents would be sold to the highest bidder. And they were.

CEO's of global juggernaut companies paid millions to have the inside track on their competitors. Secrets were stolen, plans undone and mergers destroyed; all at the hands of college age kids.

It was not until James Shriver, the main benefactor to Harrison's work, asked for a favour and the real potential of the group was realised.

Shriver had wanted inside information on a company's dealings; a company which he wanted to buy. He had all the financial records and inventory reports but those could easily be falsified or exaggerated. He wanted the real inside track. He wanted the dirt.

It was a small electronic components manufacturer but, Shriver wanted to know every little detail of the company and its staff, from the biggest regular contract, to the most insignificant supplier. Not satisfied with the operational side of the business, he also wanted the extracurricular activities of the CEO, to the petty vices of the factory janitor. Shriver wanted everything and regular covert investigation was not going to cut it.

Harrison was paid a six figure sum for the use of his lab rats. Except these lab rats didn't run around in cages. These rats ran around the deepest, darkest corners of the human mind, extracting every possible fragment of information available. Theses rats took control, changing the direction of an individual's day, with a simple thought. Unlike the white furred, pink eyed variety, these labs rats were much more difficult to control, often rebelled against some of the experiments.

But rebellion would bring harsh retribution for some.

With a successful psychic investigation of the manufacturing company for Shriver, word got round on the clandestine grapevine that existed between global companies; there were better ways to learn the secrets of another company without having to hack into their systems or bribe employees. Harrison quickly capitalised on his lab rats' skills, trying to offer their services elsewhere; untraceable infiltration from exceptional individuals.

Although they were all skilled psychics, each had very different strengths. Sometimes one Mindsweeper was preferred over another. Harrison devised a very simple code for each of the Mindsweepers.

Jamie could stay in state for such extended periods of time so he could be used for deep investigation, or remote viewing. He could infiltrate an employee's mind and stay there all day, seeing what they saw, did, and heard. Jamie was obviously given the code name SPOOK.

Jakub had the ability to taking instant control of an individual. One minute they could be walking down the street, deep in conversation, the next they could be running, fighting or doing anything he needed them to do. Of course, he would be under instructions and would have to impose another's will on an individual but he would be paid for the task and that was enough for him. The darker side to Jakub's ability was that he was a very skilled martial artist and could use another's body to conduct an attack. This made him the perfect choice for when drastic measures had to be taken. Violence was always, and often was, an option. Jakub was code named GHOST.

Miguel was a very different kind of Mindsweeper. He could remotely view all the others by stepping into their minds, seeing what they saw and influencing their decisions. He wanted control of the psychics, as much as his father had back in the seventies. He would often enter the others' minds when it was not appropriate, just to show that he could and he was chief lab rat. That is, until Roxana learned how to block him out. Because of his malevolent behaviour and frequent insubordination, he was code named ROGUE.

When it came to Roxana, she had power beyond all the others. While Spook could stay in state for an undetermined amount of time, she could go deeper. She would feel the emotion of the host. It was one thing to see and hear everything, but it was something else to become a part of the host's soul, feeling what they felt.

There were two unique elements to her power. Firstly, she could enter more than one mind at a time, taking information from the mind of one and speak it through the lips of another simultaneously. Using the skills of one individual and perform them using someone else' body, this included entering Ghost's mind and using his martial arts when needed.

The other unique element was the range of her power. All the Mindsweepers, old and new, could remote view almost anywhere in the world. The discipline took focus, with no need to enter a mind in order to 'see'. Physical control was a completely different entity. The distance between the Mindsweeper and the subject couldn't be more than a few miles and even less in a big city.

Psychic energy was much like electrical energy; the higher the concentration of power sources, the more interference that could be suffered. With more people came more energy to disrupt any clean connection. This was not a problem for Roxana; she could link and control a subject in a city as dense as London, while she herself could be standing on the bustling streets of Manhattan.

It was this power that made her the most desirable Mindsweeper to use, instant connection, anywhere in the world. This made her feared, by the mere mortals controlling the missions and Mindsweepers alike. Her power was the most difficult to explain. Even though Harrison was a scientist and could use only scientific methods to measure and record the Mindsweeper's abilities, he once stated that Roxana's power was a gift from God.

And like a messenger of God, she became known as ANGEL.

# Chapter Thirty Four

Los Angeles 2002

The dark blue Mazda MX5 Miata zipped from lane to lane. The Californian sun gleaming off the flawlessly waxed panels of the little convertible, as it accelerated passed all other traffic. The speed limit was of little importance, and law enforcement even less so.

Accidents are often caused by the unpredictable behaviour of other drivers when matched with the excess speed of another. Excess speed was not a problem when the driver could predict the movements of all the other vehicles. It was how Rogue liked to drive. Half his mind was controlling the car; the other half was in a shallow Mindsweep, drifting into the conscious minds of the drivers ahead, seeing everything they saw and sensing their movements. Driving this way was safer - in his opinion.

"Where are you taking me?" Roxana gripped the seat and forced her feet into the plush foot-well upholstery. She braced for an impact that she knew wouldn't come but the erratic driving still scared her.

"I thought you might have swept me to find out," he laughed, his eyes fixed ahead. Swept was the slang term they used. It referred to one Mindsweeper trying to read another Mindsweeper. It was frowned upon but it happened, daily.

"You're blocking me, or I wouldn't have had to ask," she had her head turned toward the teenage Rogue beside her. She wasn't looking at him but instead tried to find a way in to his head. His mind was strong but hers was superior.

She had managed to overcome the defences of both Ghost and Spook, but Rogue's mind worked in a very different way to the others. Maybe it was why he had no conscience about the things he did. Roxana always thought that Rogue couldn't have been wired up correctly by the way he tormented others.

Only a week or so ago, he had performed a Mindsweep on a homeless man, for no particular reason other than the fact that he could, and walked the man under a garbage truck. When he was asked why; 'Just to give the passengers something to talk about,' was the answer. He had little regard for human life, especially those individuals that sat somewhere outside normality. He could do it because nobody dared challenge him; nobody apart from Roxana, that is.

"So come on, where are you taking me?" she persisted.

"It's a birthday surprise for you," he smiled his perfect smile and took his eyes off the road for a second to look at his passenger.

Whatever the surprise was, she imagined it wouldn't be the nice surprise on her sweet sixteenth birthday that a normal girl with normal friends would receive.

"By surprise, you mean something I won't know about," she eyed him curiously and scanned for a chink in his mental armour, there wasn't one, "but surprises are meant to be nice, especially if they are birthday surprises. I doubt you're bringing me anywhere nice or have anything pleasant planned."

"Wait and see." he smiled again, swerving the car across all four lanes of the freeway and taking the off ramp for Beverly Hills.

The roads twisted and turned but the traffic was light. The further away from the freeway they travelled the bigger and more affluent the homes became. Hollywood paid well, the evidence was all around them. Expansive homes with a dozen bedrooms and bathrooms each, but no more than two or three regular occupants to fully immerse themselves with the excesses of the lifestyle. Olympic sized swimming pools and professional quality tennis courts, always overpriced and often underused. Triple garages that couldn't accommodate the half dozen exclusive cars that lined the uniquely paved driveways, but often housing every tool known to man, never to be used, just displayed for show. Exactly like the perfectly sculpted fountains, pillars and cloisters of the houses priced by the tens of millions of dollars, just for show, excess on top of excess.

Rogue parked up on the roadside, opposite the entrance of a gated community.

"You remember the movie we went to see last month?" he asked the confused passenger.

"Yeah, I remember it. Action picture, family held hostage. Hero had to break the law and give up his business to save them?" she replied.

"Well, you know the actor who played the double crossing partner, the one who gets shot by the wife at the end of the film?"

"Yeah, yeah, good looking guy with the sinister eyes…"

"Exactly! Well he lives just beyond those gates," he pointed to the large, ornate metalwork that separated the 'A' listers from the mere mortals.

"Really?" her face lit up with all the giddy excited glee of a fan about to meet her hero, "Why have you brought me here? Are we going to meet him? Is this my surprise?"

"Kind of…" he grinned. Not the grin of someone doing something nice for a friend but the grin of someone about to smash a dream to smithereens in the worst possible way. And enjoy doing it.

"What do you mean 'Kind of,' Miguel?" she spied him with suspicious eyes. If this was some kind of joke then it would be what was expected from Rogue, "Why are we here?"

"It's the third house on the left, with a red Ferrari on the drive. Let your mind take you there and see what's going on." The grin was fixed but his eyes were drifting toward the gates, hoping his mind would accompany her on the excursion.

"What are you up to?"

"See for yourself."

Reluctantly, Roxana drifted into a remote viewing trance. Her consciousness took her vision across the quiet suburban street and effortlessly through the locked barrier. She could see the lush greenery, smell the scented plants and feel the breeze upon her skin as though she was walking the path toward her hero's house. Her physical body was sitting in the passenger seat of the dark blue convertible. Only her mind travelled freely. She could speed up or slow down, if she so wished. View from road height or take an aerial approach, the choice was hers, such was her ability.

She was greeted by a large flagstone stone arch with remotely controlled steel gates. Just beyond was the bright red Ferrari, the paintwork glowed, sparkling from the many layers of carnauba wax reflecting the afternoon sun off the extreme curves of the Italian designed super car.

As before, her mind drifted through the gates, effortlessly, without opening them. She passed the car and up the steps, toward the large wooden front door. Slowly she eased her vision through the door, experiencing the layers of solid wood and steel reinforcements until she could see the expansive hallway. Gleaming marble floor, ornate cast iron wall art, and gently spiralling carved wooden staircase, dripped in Hollywood wealth.

Somewhere from within the house she could hear something; a disturbance, a fight or something far more sinister.

She swiftly put her viewpoint into the room where the commotion was coming from.

Now she could see and hear everything perfectly.

The actor, Roxana's hero, was standing over a woman who was sprawling on the floor between a white leather sofa and a wooden coffee table. The woman, dressed in little more than her underwear; a tight fitting white vest and a matching pair of panties covered her dignity. But dignity was not a word that could be used to describe the scene.

Tears merged with eye make-up smudged chaotically across her face. Her nose bleeding, her lip split, and a swelling on her left cheek. Fingerprint bruising lined her arms where she had been repeatedly grabbed.

"What have you been saying behind my back?" The actor screamed.

The woman just shook her head. Her mouth opening and closing but formed no words as the piteous sorrow that enveloped her, silencing any sound that dared escape.

"Are you trying to ruin me? Are you trying to take all this from me?" The actor punctuated his vicious questions with a sweeping hand, catching his helpless victim across the face.

Roxana watched as though it was a scene from a movie, but there was no camera, no sound crew, and no director coordinating the action. This was a raw moment in the life of the rich and famous; a segment of Hollywood life that nobody gets to see until it's too late.

She tried to penetrate the actor's mind but found it impossible. Maybe the rage that flowed through the man forced out any kind of outside influence, or maybe this man was an impenetrable and was impervious to any kind of attack from a Mindsweeper.

Roxana needed to do something. She couldn't watch anymore.

The actor paused in his attack. He stood over the woman, looking down at her, hate oozing from every pore. The next move was not obvious but something else was coming.

If she couldn't take the aggressor's mind then she would have to control the victim.

Roxana had had some basic martial arts training, as did all the other Mindsweepers. She never understood why until this moment.

Swiftly, she went from viewing, to a Mindsweep, putting herself in control of the victim. As two consciousness merged into one, the terrified mind of the woman spread the fear like a wild fire through every cell of Roxana's brain. The young psychic felt the woman's terror and hatred mix with adrenalin, the sense of panic was all consuming.

Roxana lashed out, using the woman's position on the floor in the best way possible. A well placed heel to the actor's kneecap brought him tumbling down. In the time it took him to fall, she was on her feet. The actor had fallen on to his back across the table, his head lolling over the edge, exposing his larynx. She punched down hard, instantly choking the man.

Roxana gauged that the woman she inhabited was physically strong. She hadn't expected such a good result from two well placed blows.

It was her turn to stand over a wounded soul now. The disgraced hero of the silver screen writhed in pain.

Her next move wasn't clear but as she became comfortable within someone else's body. The memories of the woman started to meld into Roxana's conscious mind. Recollections of past beatings and humiliation dominated. This was not a healthy relationship; it was abusive and controlling.

The distraction of the memories was all it took for the actor to regain his composure. He swiped out and took the woman's leg from under her. Roxana felt the fall but not the pain of the impact.

She was able to kick out again, this time catching the actor between his legs. He uttered a sharp yelp, much like a dog in pain. Swiftly, Roxana got the woman to her feet, this time a rage flowing through her. The mixture of the woman's memories and witnessing the level of violence overwhelmed Roxana's emotional limits. The rage turned to vengeance. The kicks continued this time, not allowing the man to recover enough to resume his attack.

A final swing of a heel stunned the actor, leaving him flat out, unable to respond.

That was all the advantage that needed to be gained.

She spied a heavy marble ashtray on the table.

It felt heavy; solid.

She brought it down, hard. Once. Twice. Three times.

Warm blood splattering the woman's face shocked Roxana, pulling her back into the moment. She dropped the stained ashtray to the floor, gazing upon the blood that covered the finely manicured hands of the woman.

What had she done?

She had saved a woman's life, that's what.

She withdrew and was instantly sitting back in the car, outside the gated community and safe from harm. She looked down at her hands. No blood. No false nails; just the bitten fingernails of a sixteen year old girl.

"I killed him!" she could barely speak.

Rogue turned around in his seat to face her.

"No, she killed him." He said with a grin.

"No, no. I killed him, I smashed his head in." Her words were laced with confusion.

"But there's no blood on your hands, is there?"

She looked again.

"It doesn't matter, I did it. I saw it. I felt her anger. I killed that man…" The sentence trailed off.

"He would have killed her if you hadn't of intervened." Rogue explained, "You saved that woman's life. You're a hero."

"I don't feel like one," there were tears in her eyes. The emotion overspill was too much. Her own emotions and those of the woman had merged, just as their minds had, but upon the break of the Mindsweep, she still had horror and rage surging through her veins.

The woman on the other hand would be standing over the dead body of her abusive 'A' list celebrity partner, wondering what the hell just happened.

"It will get easier." Rogue whispered.

"I'm not doing that again." She shook her head, not so much in protestation, but more to shake the violent thoughts from her head.

"This is what we were born to do, Roxana. Accept it."

As much as she didn't want to listen, she knew it to be true. They were different, with abilities that no one else could fathom. As a group they had been groomed from a very young age to be all knowing, all seeing, all feeling; human weapons who could kill with a simple thought. She knew that, it was impossible to escape from the truth, she would have a much more difficult job than the others. She was unique. She was powerful. And she was female; an element which would take a decade or more to realise the importance of.

# Chapter Thirty Five

After the briefest of showers, a vague attempt to rinse the captivity from her flesh, Nina swiftly dressed into practical clothing and a pair of running shoes. She didn't know whether there would be a sign from Roxana or contact from Ray, so for now, she would have to make her own way home.

She packed a handbag with her purse and passport. Her captors had taken her mobile phone and all her main credit cards. Luckily she was prepared for all eventualities and had a spare credit card in her purse and enough money to buy a ticket home, if she could get to an airport.

Just as a matter of precaution, she eased toward the front of the apartment, checking for hostiles. Although, she didn't know if she would be straying into the path of a sniper's bullet or the view of an eager henchman, with these recent events, anything was possible.

Carefully, she peered from the corner of the window.

There was a man, sat on a motorcycle, in the parking bay opposite the building. Whether it was paranoia or just the vibe she was getting, the man seemed out of place. Her hunch was that if there was a man out front, then there would have to be a man out back also.

Her already limited options seemed to be disappearing rapidly.

With that a car pulled up.

*

Ghost stepped out of the car and spoke to Rogue's man on the motorcycle. The conversation was unnecessary as he already knew the answer to his question but Ghost had to ask it anyway. It would not raise suspicions about his power with those under the pay of the higher powers. The Mindsweepers never revealed what they could do to an unknown audience, and his man was a stranger to him.

Ghost leaned into the car and passed the information to the younger cop.

"The girl is in the apartment - do you think you could follow me up and keep your hands to yourself?"

The chastised man merely grunted a response as he got out of the car. Ghost could feel that the man wanted to hurt him and would be a fool to try. A little rebellion was allowed.

Rogue, however would not have been so forgiving. Ghost would have to regain control of this situation. If not, Rogue would come and if he felt even the slightest hint of dissent, he would walk the cop right under a bus; just because he could.

The psychic and his young hired goon crossed the road toward the apartment complex.

\*

Like an electric shock, adrenaline filled every muscle fibre. Nina shook so much she feared she may pass out. There was no time to think any more. She had to act; now.

Grabbing her bag, she headed for the door.

She stopped dead in her tracks. There were footsteps just outside, in the corridor.

There was the sharp rap of a firm hand against the wooden door.

Surely they couldn't have made it to the third floor apartment already. And if they had, would they knock at all.

As tentatively as her trembling body would allow, she peered through the spyhole. She blinked and looked again. It was not the view she expected.

Against her better judgement, she opened the door. Nina's eyes had not deceived her.

This was not the salvation she was expecting, but maybe the next best thing.

# Chapter Thirty Six

Ray let the information sink in before he started to formulate his questions. If he was being honest with himself, he felt completely out of his depth with the scale of this case, coupled with the fact that Barney was not by his side to give an opinion, made the task all the more daunting.

"So how were the jobs arranged?" Ray asked after a few moments of silence.

"Just a phone call," Roxana answered.

"That simple? Surely that would be easy to detect and record?"

"Of course it would be," she explained, "but the request was simple. If there was a target in a city that needed the efforts of a particular Mindsweeper, then a call would be made and the instruction would sound like an off-hand comment,"

"Can you give me an example?"

"Sure, something like 'Would you be an ANGEL and sort out a problem for JOHN DOE from SOME COMPANY, he'll be flying into DALLAS, THURSDAY, NEXT WEEK.' That way the conversation would only be a few seconds long but in that sentence, we have the name, the company, the time, the place and the Mindsweeper that was requested to do the job," she said it as casually as if she was ordering a pizza, yet her employers would have been ordering far more than that.

Ray looked at his watch. Time was flying by and still there was no call from Hogarth.

"What can you tell me about Hogarth?" Ray needed to know how deep the man's loyalty was.

"Who?" Roxana cast a confused glance at Spook.

"Bradley Hogarth, he's Shriver's PA. He's the guy that came to my office to hire me. He's the guy that kidnapped Nina," Ray could see that the information was not sinking in. The psychics looked bewildered.

"We've never heard of a Bradley Hogarth." she spoke for them both.

He was doubly confused now. If they didn't know who the instigator of this chaos was, how was Ray supposed to. He knew that he could not trust the man but he felt a fool for believing that anything he had been told might be the truth.

"Bullshit!" The rage was restrained but ever present in Ray's voice.

"Honestly, I don't know who he is," the voice was sincere. She didn't know.

Spook sat silently but his whole demeanour said that he was hiding nothing.

Ray reached for his phone and scrolled through the pictures.

"This is a screen grab from my office CCTV system," Ray held the device toward the psychics.

It was visible. The horror emanated from their faces. Spook shrivelled back into his shell, his elongated frame seemed to diminish.

Roxana burst into tears, he mouth gasped for breath against the inconsolable shuddering of her petite frame.

"What is it?" Ray uttered.

"He's here," Roxana said the words but they were directed at Spook. He didn't respond.

"Who's here?" Ray asked again.

The colour had drained from her face. Was the news that bad? It had to be.

"Roxana," Ray asked again but with a more cautious tone, "who's here? Who's in the picture?"

"Rogue." She was broken, "Rogue is here." They were caught.

# Chapter Thirty Seven

Never before in her life had she been so happy to see another human being. Nina was stunned into silence. The question her lips dare not ask was answered by her saviour.

"I thought you could do with some help," Barney said with his signature smile and twinkling eyes. He was such a welcome sight.

Nina lunged forward and hugged the big man. His six foot four barn door proportions filled the corridor.

"They're out front but I'm not sure about the back," Nina said upon releasing him.

"Two men just entered the building at the front entrance and they're coming up the main stairwell, and there's a guy on a motorcycle, out back," he knew the score and had surveyed all possible escape routes.

"We can take the fire exit to the ground floor but we can't avoid the guys outside,"

"If we can't go round them, then we'll have to go through them," Barney said gripping her by the arm and leading her to the nearest fire exit.

Bursting through the door and onto the concrete and steel staircase, they were hit by the blinding sunlight; a stark contrast to the subtle lighting of the exclusive apartments. It was not possible to descend quietly and at speed. Time was of the essence, so they clattered down the first flight with little regard for the volume.

As Barney was about to set a foot down onto the next gantry, the fire exit door for that level opened. The younger cop stepped out with a Glock 17 firmly in his right hand.

Barney never pondered the situation. His own police and military training kicked in and he reacted instantly toward the armed man.

A debilitating right hook sent the young Spanish policeman crashing to the concrete floor. The weapon flew from his hand, bouncing down the stairs ahead of the fleeing couple.

"Nice work," Nina said as they continued down the stairs, the encounter with their pursuer merely interrupting the flow of their descent but not the speed.

"Thanks, it's not my first knock out," Barney glibly responded, pausing only to retrieve the firearm.

With each passing door they expected another assailant to appear but the path to the ground remained clear.

Keeping Nina tucked behind him, Barney crept toward the corner of the building and peered into the rear carpark.

There was a man perched astride a motorcycle with the engine running. He had clearly heard the commotion or the staircase.

"Stay behind me," Barney stepped out from the cover of the building, not waiting for a confirmation.

The man on the bike leapt from his mount, trying to pull his firearm but Barney already had him beat.

"Drop the gun and get down on the ground," Barney gestured with the muzzle of the gun just in case the man did not understand the words. He did as he was told.

Barney picked up the discarded weapon.

"Ever ridden on the back of a bike before?" He said to Nina.

"You're not serious?" She replied as she watched him cock his leg over the bike.

"My hire car is out front but so are the bad guys." He made a good point.

"Can you ride?"

"It's been a while. Get on!"

Nina climbed on behind him as he started the engine. It was a road bike, more powerful than anything Barney had ridden before.

The bike lurched forward and stalled. Barney started it again.

As he did so, the top fire exit door burst open.

"STOP!" Ghost appeared on the edge of the stairway balcony and screamed at the top of his lungs.

Without repeating the mistake again, Barney eased off the clutch, the bike pulling away smoothly. As soon as he notched up to the next gear he, the bike and Nina were gone. But their lead was only a slim one but maybe it was enough.

# Chapter Thirty Eight

The psychics had packed their bags and, following Ray, sneaked out of the hotel.

There had been a brief discussion on the next course of action. It had been agreed that Ray would put Roxana and Spook up at the apartment he shared with Nina. They could keep on running, but for how long; the net was closing in on the psychics, if they were to make any kind of stand, they might as well make it with a resourceful impenetrable by their side.

With all his resources were in and around the agency, Ray was feeling isolated and he needed the support. Although, not as isolated as Nina would be, a thousand miles away in Spain, but as a couple, they agreed that she was often better at thinking on her feet than Ray.

With the car loaded up, Ray punched 'Home' into the Satnav.

The long limbed Spook took the passenger seat, while Roxana curled up on the backseat. They hadn't even made the short trip to the M25 before both the psychics were fast asleep.

Ray switched on the radio but kept the volume low. Some low grade popular dance music whined away but was fortunately cut short for the news.

Try as he might, he could not concentrate on the news or the road. The broadcaster droned on about the latest political scandal and the death of some minor celebrity while vehicles crossed white lines; braking for no apparent reason, causing obstructions Ray was not equipped to deal with in his current state of mind. He was failing to predict the movement of the M25 traffic. How would he predict the next move of the malevolent cast of characters that hunted his passengers; he didn't know.

The Audi lurched and swerved, stirring the sleeping occupants but never waking them.

He slowed right down to cruise in the left hand lane. He hoped it would be enough to gain some focus and not kill them all. There was a lot of hectic motorway to cover before they would be close to sanctuary.

The miles crept by. With both hands firmly gripped on the steering wheel, Ray started to settle into the journey. He really wanted to call the office to see if there was any news but he knew that any developments would have already been called through to him. His mind was desperately trying to find the next logical step, just in case he had overlooked something vital.

Spook stirred and twitched in his sleep. The young homeless man was clearly suffering some kind of nightmare.

Ray thought of waking him but then thought better of it. Let sleeping dogs lie, or sleeping Mindsweepers, for that matter.

It wouldn't last long. There was a shriek from the back seat.

"BARNEY!" Roxana was launched from her sleep.

"What's wrong?" Ray's concern was carved into his face.

"Barney is with Nina." Her voice returning to a normal volume as she realised what was happening.

"How?"

"I don't know yet, but they're involved in a motorbike chase." She said incredulously.

There were no words. Ray's head tilted and turned trying to keep his eyes on the road, while his mind was elsewhere trying to work everything out. Whatever next?

# Chapter Thirty Nine

"BARNEY!" Nina screamed as the bike lurched and swerved, missing cars by mere inches.

She clung onto the large man for dear life. Nina trusted him but knew that he was not an experienced biker. Her eyelids squeezed tight, trying to block out her fear. It didn't help.

Barney didn't react to her screams. He focused on getting through the busy Spanish traffic. A glance in the mirror revealed the other motorcycle rider weaving a path expertly through an array of vehicles and gaining.

The man on the bike would soon be upon them. And he wasn't alone.

Steadily dodging and weaving a route through the varying speed traffic, was the remainder of the pursuing pack.

Barney couldn't make out how many there were in the car but he hoped that he and Nina could outrun them in the city traffic, giving themselves a vital head start to the airport.

As the volume of vehicles eased off, he grew more confident, accelerating on the ever clearing roads.

Speed limits were going to be broken today. It would be necessary if they were to escape.

The pitch of the motorcycle engine rose with the speed but there was the sound of another engine, closing in. The other motorcycle had also broken away from the confinement of the traffic and was drawing in.

Barney shot a look over his right shoulder to see their pursuer pulling alongside with a pistol in his hand.

Swerving into the other bike was out. The other guy was far more proficient and stopping would be to give up too easily. There were no alternatives.

Without warning, he could feel one the handguns that he had tucked into the waistband of his trousers, being removed. The python like grip on his torso eased off. He could feel movement behind him.

Nina let go with her right arm, pointing the gun at the other motorcycle as it tracked a parallel course. Two rounds exited the weapon rapidly, the bike disappearing from view.

Not sure as to what had just occurred, Barney almost turned completely around on the bike to see what had happened.

The rider lay dead, his bike discarded at the edge of the road.

An advantage gained, Barney tried to put as much distance between them and the other pursuers. Now they had a chance, a slim one, but a chance all the same.

# Chapter Forty

He had been watching in the rear-view mirror as Roxana drifted into a trance, causing him to nearly crash into a slowing vehicle. Ray was focusing on the woman behind him, not the road ahead. He pulled onto the hard shoulder.

"What's happening?" Ray urged but the psychic was still coming out of her trance.

"Let her be," Spook said in his timid voice, "she's helping them."

The seconds passed like hours. Eventually, she opened her eyes to be greeted by both men in the front seats staring back at her in anticipation.

"Well?" Ray's patience was fraying.

"Ghost and his men are chasing them," she said it as if it was the most normal thing in the world. But in her world it was normal. Psychics, espionage, strategic kidnapping and assassination; all part of the life they had lived for too many years.

"How are you helping them?"

"I just shot one of the pursuers. It will give them a head start. We need to stop somewhere quieter than here so *we* can link," Roxana pointed at Spook, "If we're to help, we need a better place than next to a busy road."

Ray asked nothing more. Gunning the engine the tyres bit into the gritted hard shoulder. Now he had a focus. Get off the motorway, get somewhere quiet, and get Nina and Barney the help they needed.

The powerful Audi cleaved a path through the traffic. Ray overtook and undertook, not caring for the rules of the road, just anxious to get to the services, only a few miles ahead.

The traffic flowed along steadily but it was still too slow for Ray. He accelerated to an unsafe speed as he saw the one mile sign for the services. With just a few hundred yards to the slip road, Ray took the car back onto the hard shoulder, flooring it past some vehicles that were being driven within the confines of the law.

Even in the services carpark, Ray ignored the 10mph speed limit; flying over speed humps designed to slow him down.

He parked up in the far corner of the overflow carpark and switched off the engine. The car was just far enough away from the road to mute motorway traffic sufficiently.

Without a word Spook jumped out of the car, climbing into the back with Roxana. The pair instantly closed their eyes, drifting into their trancelike states.

Ray could do nothing but watch and wait.

# Chapter Forty One

The gap between Barney and Nina, and their pursuers had been extended but it all could change in an instant. Once they arrived at the airport there would only be a few minutes for them to get through the check in and get lost, somewhere in the Malaga Terminal.

Barney pulled up in the taxi rank directly outside the terminal entrance.

Nina hopped off, clearly relieved to be safely standing on terra firma once more. Looking into the distance, she was confused but somewhat relieved to see there was no sign of Ghost and his henchmen.

The pair rushed through the doors.

There were only a few people in the queue, but as with most airport check-in desks, progress was slow.

Barney tapped his feet in frustration at the dawdling pace. He kept glancing at his watch, willing time to slow down whilst at the same time praying that the queue would speed up.

Nina's eyes were over her shoulder, constantly looking at the door. At any moment she expected to see their pursuers barging through the airport entrance, guns drawn and out for vengeance.

They stepped forward one more place. No gun toting bad guys suddenly appeared.

Normally, there would be small talk but the fear of capture halted any conversation, making the wait seem even longer.

Eventually they were next in line. Barney looked at his watch again, ten minutes had passed since they had arrived at the airport and there was still no sign of unfriendly faces. Maybe they had been involved in an accident. Maybe they had shot past the airport, thinking it too obvious a place for escape.

The fact that they were being pursued by psychics with an agenda had not escaped them at all. Those that followed had more advantages than disadvantages. Why had they not made an appearance?

The check-in was now clear. They both approached the counter, passports in hand.

"I've two seats booked on the next flight to Bristol under the name Barnett," Barney tried to appear calm but he could feel his voice tremble under the surge of adrenaline. He wasn't afraid, not for himself, he wanted to get Nina back in one piece to put Ray's mind at ease. How easy that would be from here, in this situation, was anybody's guess. But a corpse on a Spanish highway and a pursuing pack of grunts were variables that Barney couldn't calculate for.

The attendant took his credit card and processed the transaction with little conversation.

Nina kept her eyes on the entrance, awaiting Ghost and associates to erupt through the door.

"They should have caught up by now," Nina said, her voice hushed as though to speak a decibel louder would draw the attention they were desperately trying to avoid.

"I know." Barney replied, "I have a very bad feeling about this."

The attendant handed over two boarding passes and bid them a pleasant flight. Swiftly, Barney and Nina headed for the security check-in. Their luck still seemed to be holding as they passed through all the checks without a hitch, making their way into the bustling heart of the airport. It was time to get lost.

# Chapter Forty Two

"I don't know about you, but I could do with a drink," Nina prompted as they passed the Airport bar.

"Ditto that," Barney never needed to be asked twice, "I'll call Ray from the bar - if I can reach him."

"He's with the other Mindsweepers,"

"How do you know that?"

"Because the one called Roxana has contacted me," Nina made the statement with a wry smile on her face.

"Contacted you?" Barney seemed perplexed.

"Yeah, telepathically." She said, "It's kind of freaky."

"I bet."

"But also comforting; it was as though she could feel all my emotions and control them. When she was in my head I didn't fell frightened or alone." Nina's expression was one of wonderment, as though she was remembering some long forgotten euphoric experience.

She took a seat at an empty table whilst Barney ordered some drinks. There weren't many places to hide until their flight left so they both considered staying in public view could just be enough protection; maybe.

The airport bar had a few scattered travellers. Some nervously sipping on a little Dutch courage for their return flights; others merely passing the time whilst reminiscing on the fun they had had.

The entire time, Nina scanned the crowds but all she could see was the multitude of over tanned holiday makers heading back to their home countries.

Barney returned, placing a large white wine in front of her. He took the chair opposite Nina, his large frame looking awkward perched on a white faux leather low backed chair.

"What do we do now?" Nina asked.

"Wait for the flight," Barney's answer interrupted the big swig he was taking from his continental lager, "it's all we can do for now."

They made polite conversation until the call for their flight. The events of the last few days were just too bizarre to talk about. Nina's only question about the situation was to ask after Ray and how he was coping.

"He's been better," Barney said draining the remains of his second glass of beer mid-sentence, "his mind is shot to pieces with worry about you."

"Bless him," she said it with the fondness that only lovers can have, even though it was *her* who had been kidnapped, "I can't wait to see him."

"Well, let's hope I can get you home without too much trouble,"

"Ray wouldn't be happy if you didn't," Nina afforded a giggle as she finished her wine.

"He doesn't even know I'm here,"

Her raised brows were enough of a question.

"I caught the first flight out as soon as Ray left for Croydon," Barney gave the tell-tale wink that he usually demonstrated when he was up to something that Ray knew nothing about.

They left the glasses on the table and headed toward the gate for their flight. On the outside, they looked like tourists making their way home, but on the inside they felt like a pair of fugitives who were on the run.

Anticipation rose as they approached the gate. They could see the queue for the flight. Dozens of weary travellers, laden with hand luggage and/or excitable children, filed toward the waiting flight attendants.

They could see the plane with the attached tunnel that would bring them on-board.

They could see it all just metres in front of them.

What they did not see was the drawn automatic pistols pointing at their backs. It was only when the muzzle of one was jabbed into Barney's back that they realised the game was afoot.

He turned to see Ghost flanked by the two Spanish police officers, who were now back in their uniforms.

"Come with us," the instruction was simple and direct but impossible to ignore looking down the barrel of a gun.

Barney and Nina were ushered away from the salvation of their flight. Their fate was now in question.

# Chapter Forty Three

Roxana shuddered out of the trance. A gaunt veil of distress shrouded her exquisite face.

"What is it?" Ray asked. He was prepared for the worst but hoped for the best.

The psychic composed herself before answering. She laid a hand upon her companion in trace, to rouse him, before she spoke.

Spook opened his eyes. The same despair was all too apparent in his features.

"Ghost has them both." The words Ray did not want to hear fell from Roxana's lips.

"Has 'them'?" Ray questioned, "Are they ok? Are they hurt?"

"They're unharmed but being held at gunpoint." There was nothing of comfort in the answer.

"Can you do anything?"

Roxana understood what she was being asked but was unsure if the answer would be acceptable. She knew that Ray wanted her to get inside the mind of one or all of the captors. Yes, she had done it earlier that day but it had been a quick reaction to a dangerous situation. Roxana had done what was necessary to get Nina out. A link over such a distance would always be exhausting and often difficult to repeat, but now, Ghost would have anticipated the ability of the superior psychic, blocking her out of the henchmen's minds, in much the same way Roxana had locked everyone out of Nina's mind.

Roxana's ability was untouchable in close proximity but at the distance in question, she would be unable to break through her opposing colleague's handy work.

"Not from here." Was all she could say.

Ray didn't reply. He started the engine and headed out of the services.

As they entered the roundabout to bring them back onto the motorway, Roxana sat bolt upright in the back of the car.

"They are coming here."

"What do you mean?" Ray nearly drove the car off the road, almost turning completely around in the driver's seat.

"They are going to be boarding a private jet and heading back to the UK" She smiled as the news was delivered but maybe a smile wasn't entirely appropriate.

"When?" Ray asked.

"Right now."

The information brought some hope with it. With both his business partner, and his life partner, heading back to home soil, Ray felt motivated to gain control of the situation. He would, at all costs. He had to.

# Chapter Forty Four

Barney was ushered into a private room with the muzzle of the handgun pressed firmly into the small of his back.

Nina followed timidly. Her heart racing as the hand of the older cop pressed against the nape of her neck, guiding her in the same direction. The last time his hand was upon her, was a violation, this time, with a weapon held against her was terrifying.

The group passed through the dividing door and into a large private hangar. Standing at the top of a galvanised metal gantry, they looked down over a private jet, bright white with SAED emblazoned across the fuselage in pale blue lettering. The high pitched whine of the engines were deafening within the confines of the steel building.

"What now?" Defiance over spilled into Barney's words.

"We are going back to the UK," Ghost began.

"Well, we don't need a ride. We already have flights booked,"

Ghost flinched at the interruption.

"Mr Barnett, if I were you, I would be quiet," his Polish accent seemed to become more noticeable with the anger rising in his voice.

"I suppose I should as you have all the guns…" Barney's words were cut short.

"Barney, please…" Nina interjected trying to calm the situation.

"Listen to your friend, Barney," Ghost laughed over the nickname, "and maybe we will not have to shoot you,"

"If you insist,"

"I do," without warning, Ghost pulled a Taser from his jacket pocket and prodded it into Barney's armpit. He dropped to the floor, his muscular body taut from the numbing flow of electricity.

Ghost took the handgun from the younger cop's hand and pointed it at Nina. He then gestured to his henchmen to pick up the fallen detective.

"I trust I have your cooperation?" Ghost asked.

Nina slowly nodded. She didn't want to chance a remark that saw her stunned again and did as she was asked.

Together they clanked down the steel staircase toward their flight. Nina led the way with Ghost loosely aiming the gun at her back. It was not the way the psychic was used to killing people, the weapon looked uncomfortable in his hand.

Ghost preferred to use another's hands to commit his crimes. To him it was the disassociation from the act that justified it in his mind. He was not comfortable with taking life without a valid reason. Up until now, all his targets had been sanctioned by a higher power; a power that paid well and gave justifiable reasons for its actions.

This job, however, was sanctioned by Rogue. There was no pay, only an obligation to a colleague. Ghost would fulfil that obligation but not out of loyalty; out of fear of Rogue.

As the group neared the plane, the two cops stumbled and nearly dropped the unconscious Barney. His heavy physique proved difficult to carry.

The younger cop made a comment under his breath in his native Spanish to his law enforcement colleague. The older cop agreed.

"I have said before, I may not speak your language but I know what you are saying," Ghost snapped.

Nina afforded a smile, it was far from a situation for levity, but it was a possible anecdote for the future if they ever got out of the predicament. She was fluent in Spanish, overhearing the grumble of the younger cop, who thought it would have been better to have Tasered the big guy after they had gotten him on to the plane. Nina agreed, silently.

"Just get him on the plane and bind his hands." Ghost's patience was wearing thin with his hired help.

"What are we going back to?" She asked as she too was ushered onto the plane.

"Rogue," Ghost swallowed as he uttered the name, as if the very mention of it stuck in his throat, "Rogue is waiting for all of us,"

"All of us?"

"Yes, all of us; Roxana, Spook, and Mr Dean too,"

There was no reply from the terrified Nina. She pondered the thought of how evil must Rogue be if someone like Ghost was frightened of him. Maybe she could warn Ray via the female psychic but perhaps the message would not get through, not because the psychic wouldn't receive it because maybe it was part of an elaborate trap. Nina didn't know what to think anymore.

# Chapter Forty Five

They were on the move again. Inside the car there was silence but Ray's head was screaming with questions. Questions, he was too scared to ask, with answers, too daunting to hear.

Both Roxana and Spook were huddled onto the back seat. Her eyes were closed but her head was not resting against anything. Ray guessed that she might be in one of her trances, as her stance was too rigid for sleep.

Spook had managed to fit his long spindly legs behind the front seat and had fallen asleep already; his head lolling against the rear pillar of the car as he was too tall for the head rest.

"Are you awake?" Ray broke the silence.

Roxana's eyes opened immediately. It was almost as though she had been waiting for nothing else but the questions, surprised that it had taken so long for them to be asked, but ready all the same.

"Yes," she answered curiously.

"Were you in one of your trances?"

"I was,"

"Is there anything happening that I should know about?" Ray almost wished he wasn't an impenetrable so that she could read the questions directly from the centre of his anxious brain and give fully detailed answers. But that wasn't going to happen.

"The jet is taxiing at the moment. Nina and Barney are on board, unharmed, although Barney has been bound and stunned. He's the boisterous one, isn't he?"

"He is that." Ray said with a sad smile. He knew that Barney was his own worst enemy sometimes; fearless but foolhardy.

"Well, I've blocked his mind so that neither Ghost nor Rogue can get in. Is there anything else you wish to ask?" Roxana anticipated there were a million and one questions to follow but they had time to kill. She needed to tell the story; the whole story.

"Did you kill Shriver?"

The duration of the pause said far more than any words that followed. Ray wasn't a psychic. He wasn't trained by an ex-CIA stooge. He wasn't doing parlour tricks for money. But he could see the answer carved into the stone expression on the young woman's face.

Ray didn't think for one second that he would be able to comprehend the lives of the occupants of his backseat. Gifted orphans, taken and trained to manipulate others, spy for corporate greed and kill without question. If their lives took a more normal path from hereon, they would still be damaged beyond belief. Who would know how they could move forward from here. Ray certainly didn't.

"What do you think?" Her question was deliberate and measured.

Ray sighed at her reply giving his own hypothetical answer.

"The length of time it took you to answer suggests that 'yes' you did. I imagine you had a very good reason to do so and I'd like to know why," he paused briefly before finishing his exchange, "Is that fair?"

"Since I was a small child, I have been pushed and prodded, examined and experimented on. You don't know how completely lost you are until someone thinks they can profit from you. I have been a commodity for my whole life, sold to the highest bidder for my skills. I feel like a prostitute and THEY were my pimps. Not selling my body - selling my mind." Tears graced her smooth olive cheeks but the words continued, spat from her mouth with the bitter taste that only exploitation can generate, "They didn't care how I felt about it. They didn't care how devastating it feels to enter somebody's mind, see their whole life, see everything that they had to lose and then take it from them. I'm not only crying for myself but for all those that I've killed at the request of others. Shriver may have looked like a generous man; a benevolent man, but he was worse than Harrison or Rogue for what he wanted from me."

Ray watched in the rear-view mirror as her shoulders shuddered, sobbing replacing the sour words that had fallen so easily from her lips. He despaired for her. She hadn't asked for this life but it was thrust upon her anyway.

The Audi drifted through the traffic with ease as they left the M25. The miles seemed to melt away steadily; the Satnav counting down the distance to whatever awaited them. After what Ray thought was an appropriate amount of time, he asked the most painful question.

"You said they wanted something from you," Ray watched as her eyes locked his via the mirror, clearly anticipating the inevitable, *"what did they want?"*

"My baby,"

"You have a child?" His pitch rose with surprise.

"I'm pregnant. In my first trimester," Roxana saw the confusion in his eyes, "about twelve weeks to you."

"Why do they want your baby?"

"Because it's a pure bred psychic baby!" Bitter sarcasm replaced the sorrow in her voice.

Before he could ask the how and who, she started to spill the whole saga to him.

In her life she hadn't met many people she could trust. Her ability gave her too many insights into other's thought processes, especially in the covert world, where she and her other psychic brethren inhabited. Roxana knew how genuine a person was. It took no effort for her, if that person was in the same room, to see their cogs working. She could see their thoughts form as though they were her own. Whether it was goodwill or deception, it mattered not. There wasn't much that she could not see or feel.

Ray was an enigma to her. Impenetrables were much rarer than psychics, if the truth be told, but even those with a figuratively bulletproof psyche could be read to a degree, even if they couldn't be controlled.

That day in Croydon when the two drunken men attacked her, she couldn't penetrate the older man fully but she could see the intent materialise in his thoughts. Ray was different, she could not see, feel or read anything from him. But strangely, she trusted him. When she had linked with Nina, Roxana could feel the trust that the kidnapped woman had for her man. She could feel the love, sense the respect, and suffer the separation that only someone in love could experience. This made Ray the man that she could tell her story to.

She had never felt love before. Not in the romantic sense. The closest she had ever been to another human being was with Spook. And that was more akin to a big sister role. She had felt Spook's pain. Experienced the suffering through his nightmares and knew that his life, as a psychic, was very different from hers.

Whilst she could keep her mind separate, for the most part, from the mind she intruded on, Spook could not. As powerful as his ability was, he lived his intrusive psychic connections through the very darkest thoughts of the host mind. This meant that he felt the anguish of everyone that he had entered and experienced it first-hand. While in trance he lived in the most terrifying depths of the human condition. So much so, that he carried that agony into his own world. Spook had lived the most harrowing existences of more people than he could remember. His life was a torment, constantly.

And while she trusted Spook, she couldn't reveal the things that were happening to her. His sensitive heart and delicate mind were too fragile to understand that the person he could most rely on for strength and support was actually more vulnerable than she allowed anyone to see.

Spook didn't know she was pregnant. Until she told Ray, only two others knew of her condition, James Shriver and Rogue. Their reasons for knowing were the most disturbing.

From the very early years of the psychic development program, whether government or corporate funded, Marcus Harrison, the father figure to all the orphaned psychics, wanted to discover the psychic gene. To discover whether the most miniscule fragment of the human genome was responsible for the gifts the orphans displayed.

Samples were taken, cultivated and studied, but the results were inconclusive. Harrison needed to find the gene that made the difference between these 'super' psychics and everybody else.

Shriver needed more. As he was funding all of Harrison's research, he wanted a financial benefit to his investment. Contracting out the abilities of four gifted individuals was a source of income but nothing like the value of the ability itself. Shriver wanted to sell the gene to the highest bidder. The military implications were unparalleled, but the samples of genetic information were not tangible enough for the foreign powers prepared pay millions, maybe even billions, for such a powerful commodity.

What Shriver sought to create, with or without Harrison's help, was a pure bred psychic child with stem cells and DNA for sale to the highest bidder. This is where Rogue came in.

Roxana was a beautiful woman; petite, dark skinned, jet black hair and stunning eyes. She had been courted and pursued by many men, from her time as a student, to the period spent working within Shriver's offices; she always turned heads. Both men and women gazed upon her with desire; but no one more so than Rogue.

While she did date and exchanged kisses with those she found herself attracted to, not a single man could win her over to take that step beyond her bedroom door. She had intruded into the minds of too many broken hearted women and too many trophy chasing men, to allow herself to be drawn in to an area never explored - her own feelings. Approaching her thirtieth birthday, she had maintained her virginity. Roxana had always thought, in her own time, she would meet someone who would make her life seem as though it was her own, someone who wouldn't exploit her for her ability; loved her for who she really was and not the lost orphan yearning to be loved that she used to be. She longed for that day when she would be bonded to another human being, and not via a psychic link. Well that time was now.

Growing within her womb was the only person who would be genetically related to her, that she would ever remember meeting. Her wish had come true but not in the manner that anyone would want for the creation of a new life. The child's conception was a violation by one of her own.

Three months previously, Roxana had been at the Shriver building, working late at her cover story job, in the orphan charity office. The corporate use of the psychics had been dwindling of late and the contracts were not coming in as they had been. Even after Spook's departure a year previously, the work for three was pretty thin on the ground.

Shriver wanted to somehow showcase his assets and get the programme back on track. His plan was to expand his company exponentially, to make a statement to those within the Fortune 500 business sector, suggesting that he could provide the same level of success to already lucrative enterprises with a longer term incentive.

Not only would Shriver provide the full use of *his* psychics, he would furnish the company with their own tailor made genetically enhanced and fully trained psychic of their own. The only problem was, no such psychics existed, as yet. He needed to provide one, quickly.

Knowing that Roxana would not agree in being the handmaiden to Shriver's sick dream, Rogue decided to take the step that he had read from Shriver's own mind.

On that fateful night, Roxana had just returned home to her apartment, where she had lived alone, since Spook had left, and decided to get in an early night. After a sandwich and a glass of milk, she took a shower, changed for bed, and crashed out in front of the TV.

A psychic's mind is a turbulent place to dwell. Spook had never been able to switch off his mind but that was down to the influence Rogue had had over him. The others had to find their own ways of switching off the pathways that gave them their power. Roxana would often watch TV to fill her mind with other things, allowing her to zone out. But zoning out also made her vulnerable, especially to a low moral individual such as Rogue.

As the TV movie that she had been watching was coming to an end, Roxana could feel herself drifting toward sleep. The leaden weights that pulled at her lids also seemed to pin her to the sofa. *'Just for a few minutes'* was the thought barely keeping her conscious but that was all it was, a thought. Soon her eyes were closed, the ending of the film was missed and forgotten.

As sleep deepened, her mind became wide open. Thoughts twisted and turned through the spiralling vortex of her unconsciousness. Dreams were formed and lost. Fragments of days gone by appeared and were swiftly banished, as other more attractive images entered her head. Faces of people, long since forgotten, swirled into focus only to be shattered by the unseen breeze that flowed amid the serotonin creating her dreams.

One face kept returning, remaining in focus longer than all the others before vanishing. It was the face of Kyle, her high school sweetheart. The only man she could claim she almost loved. He was tall, handsome and athletic; all the things a high school kid should be. His perfect blond hair, deep blue eyes and flawless complexion wrapped around a model's bone structure, meant he could also turn heads. But only Roxana could turn his. She smiled in her slumber, letting out a deep sigh of satisfaction. In an empty room it would not have mattered. In her apartment in which she believed she was alone, it should not have mattered. But she was not alone. She was sinking into an erotically charged dream, with one that coveted her, gazing at her lithe, nubile body covered in only a thin T-shirt.

Rogue's eyes absorbed every curve, every line and every movement. Soon he would have what he desired most and then Shriver would have what he desired.

# Chapter Forty Six

The lurch of the small, banking aircraft was enough to wake Barney from his stunned slumber. The last thing he remembered was pushing the boundaries of his captor's tolerance. Now he was strapped into the seat of a private jet with his hands bound by a cable tie.

"Are you ok?" Nina was sat opposite. Her seatbelt still fastened but she didn't have the added cable tie.

"I think so," he took a cursory look at his surroundings. The two armed cops were sitting at the opposite end of the passenger compartment, talking. Ghost, on the other hand was nowhere to be seen, "didn't you think to karate chop the bad guys in the throat and make a break for it?"

Nina flashed a sarcastic smile in his direction.

"Sorry, I didn't think it was my place to rescue the knight in shining armour," she glanced up and down at his attire of a t-shirt and a pair of cargo pants, "or a knight in double khaki,"

"Nice," Barney knew Nina was wise to his banter, "so what's the plan?"

"You tell me. Didn't you come with a plot to rescue?"

"Nah, not really, I came on an impulse. Get here. Help you. Tell Ray nothing."

"Why?"

"I figured they would be keeping an eye on you and Ray and wouldn't bother with me..."

"And you would be correct, Mr Barnett," The unmistakable accented drawl of Ghost fired over his head.

The psychic left his seat and took the one next to Barney.

"It's always the details, ain't it." Barney wasn't about to tone down his lack of respect for his captors.

"Indeed," Ghost nodded his head, "but rest assured that we will not make that mistake again,"

"Did you know, the calmer you are, the better your English is."

"And did you know, you are a better travel companion when you are unconscious." Ghost pulled the Taser from his pocket and waved it in Barney's face.

Barney shut up.

"What are you going to do with us?" Nina asked, trying to deflect the attention from her friend's petulant behaviour.

"That is not my decision or your concern at this time."

"It is our concern, but whose decision is it?" Nina wasn't about to quit with the questions.

"Rogue," Ghost's voice trembled as he uttered the name, "Rogue will know what to do with you."

"You're scared of him aren't you?" Barney asked. This time there was no hint of defiance in his tone.

"He is someone to be scared of." The air of superiority was lost from the Mindsweeper's voice.

"And who is he scared of?" Barney chanced another question.

The answer was not what Barney or Nina was expecting.

"Roxana; He's scared of Roxana."

The conversation ended there.

# Chapter Forty Seven

Roxana hadn't paused for breath. She had been recalling the most appalling moment of her life with resounding dignity. Before that critical day, Roxana had thought nothing of violating somebody's mind, taking their thoughts and controlling their will. It was what she had been brought up to do. It was normal to her, not right, but she knew that too.

Once she had been violated, the game had changed. Not only had her mind been violated but her body too. She was now compelled to feel empathy with all the people whose mind's that she had invaded. While some had deserved the mental intrusion, many had been innocent; manipulated for the gain of others.

Ray sat behind the wheel of his car, steering his way through the traffic but barely conscious of it all. His mind was a maelstrom of Roxana's tragic life. The details of which were far too awful to contemplate. Innocence lost for commodity's sake.

"Rogue raped you?" He had to ask to be clear.

"I didn't consent to it so, yes, he raped me," the words that confirmed the act brought the tears "he invaded my mind, planted a dream to make me responsive and took what he wanted."

"Evil. Utterly evil,"

"He is evil, he has been top dog in the programme for so long that he gets his way, every time,"

"I thought you were the most powerful," Ray was confused.

"I am, but like so many avenues of life, it's a man's world. My ability is nothing compared to Rogue's influence over the programme. Harrison runs after him like a spoilt child. Shriver uses him as the poster boy for his evil deeds and Ghost looks up to him like a big brother but fears him all the same."

"What about Spook?" Ray couldn't help but notice that the tall and gangly psychic sitting as upright as he could in the confined space of the backseat, listening to the tale, "Why is he not influenced in any way?"

"Because he's mine," Roxana cast a loving gaze at her companion, "he helps me and I help him. Rogue tortured him so much that he had to leave for his own sake."

"Why didn't you go too?"

"You make it sound like it was a choice. Do you not understand the kind of people you are dealing with? They kill to get their way. Trust me when I say that Rogue will not hesitate to kill you, Nina or Barney. In fact that's part of the reason he's here in person."

Ray jerked on the steering wheel. The Audi lurched from the middle lane, across the left-hand lane, almost hitting another car, screeching to a halt on the gritty surface of the hard shoulder.

"What the fuck did you just say?" The lost, timid side that Ray had made all too obvious was gone, the raging investigator that he so often was, had returned.

She could feel his anger. Not because she could read him now, but because he gave her no choice, enveloping her with his rage.

"He came for me and my child but he also came for you." Now she was timid.

"What does he want with me?"

"He holds you responsible for the death of his father." She could feel his breath on her face. He had not only turned in his seat but Ray had almost forced himself into the back seat, so much was his determination for an acceptable answer.

Ray paused in confusion, trying to construct the pieces of the puzzle.

"His father has been dead thirty years; killed by one too many experiments in his quest for some kind of god-like power. I didn't kill him, he killed himself."

"His father's mind lived on in Edward Langston. You know that."

"I do, but Langston took his own life. I merely witnessed his death." Ray's anger subsided. His rage was not for the frightened, pregnant woman perched in the back of his car, but for the psychopathic son of a dead psychic.

"It was you that outed him," Roxana composed herself, "he holds you responsible for the discovery and eventual death."

"What about Nina and Barney?"

"They were part of the discovery - their names are in all the articles on the internet. Part of Rogue's plan is to remove all the references to The Mindsweeper Project, good or bad. That is, after he's removed all of you." She told of the plan as if it was an after dinner anecdote. The truth was she was used to these types of plans, although never before had she blown the whistle so spectacularly.

"I'm not going to make it easy for him." The adrenalin flowed through his veins, igniting the flame of his defiant streak.

"He has your girlfriend and your partner. He's holding all the cards."

Ray pondered that suggestion for a moment, sitting back in to the driving seat. Three people sat in perfect silence, one considering a plan; the other two were in uncharted territory. Usually they would know everything by now, but with this impenetrable man, they could only guess.

The car shook with the shockwave of each passing car. Minutes ticked by. Minutes they didn't have. Somewhere, an aircraft was drawing nearer to its destination and they were heading nowhere.

Ray looked over his shoulder to see pensive faces looking back.

"He's not holding all the cards."

"What do you mean?" She quizzed.

"I've got an ace of my own." a wry smile spread across his face.

Roxana and Spook exchanges glances, they didn't need to speak, they knew each other's thoughts as well as they knew their own, neither could fathom Raymond Dean's thinking.

"What ace?" Roxana shook her head as she asked the question.

"You!" he pointed directly at her, "You're my ace. He wants you and your child, and I want Nina and Barney. If he wants you, he's gonna have to trade."

"Are you serious? Don't think he's just going to give them up because he won't. And even if he does, do you think that will be the end of it? Rogue will never give up. If he wants you dead then you are going to have to kill to stop him."

"I'm not him. I don't kill people." Doubt crept into Ray's head for a second.

"I know that but you're underestimating how ruthless he is." Roxana had real concern emblazoned across her face for Ray's naivety.

"And you are underestimating me."

Those were to be the last words spoken in the car for some time. Ray re-joined the motorway and headed back to Bristol. Whatever the outcome when they arrived, somebody's misjudgement would be revealed. And the consequences would be deadly.

# Chapter Forty Eight

The aircraft banked, adjusting in the air for its final approach, the pitch of the engines lowering as they were powered down. The deceleration could be felt by all on board, as the vibrations resonated through the fuselage.

Nina and Barney sat grim faced, opposite each other, their seatbelts on.

Barney watched the descent from the small porthole windows of the private jet. He observed a motorway, the M5 he presumed, and a raft of industrial structures. Every now and again he would catch a glimpse of a familiar building, but he couldn't be sure as he was seeing them from an unfamiliar angle.

"The city looks so different from here." he thought out loud.

"They all look different from the air, dummy." Nina afforded a smile at the comment.

"I get that, but I know this place better than anywhere else and it just seems so different, almost unrecognisable."

"You've flown into Bristol before, surely?"

"Yeah, to the airport, but I feel like we are going to land in a field any minute."

Ghost entered from the rear cabin.

"We are going to be landing very soon," Ghost was nervous. His Eastern European accent was significantly more apparent, "Rogue will be waiting for us,"

"Will Ray be there?" Nina asked. Her voice also broke with the anticipation of what was to come.

"I'm not sure." The confusion was very obvious on the young man's face. A psychic he may have been, but knowledgeable he was not.

"Why don't you know?" Barney's sarcasm dripped from his words, "All good little henchmen should know the plan."

"I still have the Taser," Ghost was not amused.

"It's all you have." Was his final reply.

He powered the Taser into Barney's leg and the big man shuddered, violently, before sinking lifelessly back into the seat, once the power had been cut.

"You friend does not learn, does he?" He walked away not waiting for a reply.

Ghost took his seat just as the small craft decelerated again for the final approach.

Nina sat in silence for the landing. The aircraft rumbled onto the runway and lurched under breaking. Of all the times she had landed back in the UK, this was the only time she wouldn't know who would be greeting her.

From the window she could see several large hangars, some offices, a refuelling truck, and a commercial airliner parked in a siding. This wasn't so much a private airfield but more an industrial facility with a runway.

The jet taxied toward one of the smaller hangars. It rolled through the open end of the building, stopping sharply just inside.

Nina looked over her shoulder toward the front of the cabin and kicked Barney at the same time, trying to wake him.

The door opened but nobody disembarked. Instead someone slowly climbed the short staircase into the plane. Nina didn't recognise him. The others merely nodded a welcome.

The man in a suit, with sharp, tanned features smiled as he walked toward her.

"Pleased to meet you Miss Fuller," a hand shot in her direction.

Nina took it but her trepidation was clear.

"Who are you?" She asked.

"Hogarth…" Barney answered. He was conscious.

"I'm afraid not Mr Barnett." He cast the briefest of glances toward the big man before turning his attention back to her, "My name is Miguel Sanchez but you can call me, Rogue."

The colour drained from Nina's face as she heard that surname, realising the full weight of their predicament.

# Chapter Forty Nine

Back on familiar territory, Ray pulled off the motorway and found a truck stop. He parked up right in the centre of the car park and switched off the engine.

"We are miles from anywhere so I would advise you not to run. I'm going to make a phone call but I won't be far away. Please sit tight." Ray communicated his wishes and got out of the car, removing his car keys as he left.

His legs felt heavy after such a tense drive. He stretched openly in the middle of the car park, not caring who could see him, in reality there were only the occupants of his Audi and the bored looking burger van man to witness anything at all.

Pulling his phone from a jacket pocket, Ray could see there were a number of missed calls, texts and voicemails, but only the ones from Hogarth and from his office were of any real interest. He smiled at the name HOGARTH all in capitals spread across his screen. It was not a nice smile.

He wondered what name he would have to use; Hogarth, Sanchez or Rogue.

Ray tapped on Hogarth's voicemail and raised the phone to his ear. As he waited for the message to start he afforded a cursory look back at his car to check that there were still two figures in the back seat. There was. He locked the car and turned away as the elongated drawl of the despotic psychic relayed the instructions.

When the message ended, Ray immediately tapped on Pete's name. The call was answered within three rings.

"What gives boss?" Pete was never formal.

"I've been given my orders."

"Have you still got the Mindsweepers?"

"I have."

"What's the next move?"

"I need a favour from you." Ray was concerned about Pete's willingness after the whole Mindsweeper saga the previous year.

"What is it?" Pete's tone was cautious.

Ray gave a detailed plan of what he would like to happen next and how Pete could play his part. There was a lot of assumption and guesswork but the plan could not involve the psychics. Trust was something Ray didn't have for anybody but his own team, and even that could be undone with the intervention of those with the ability to control minds.

Ray was at the mercy of all the unknown factors but he had to stay in control. An inch given to Rogue could be more than enough to undo everything.

With the instructions delivered he hung up on Pete. He scrolled to the HOGARTH entry in his contacts list. Tapping on the name, he waited for the call to connect. What happened next would be critical; life changing in fact.

# Chapter Fifty

The disembarking was unlike any other flight they had ever been on. Nina had been ushered off the plane at gun point, although a gun was quite unnecessary. She would have left the aircraft willingly; sprinted and never stopped until this saga was a distant memory.

One of the Spanish henchmen told her to sit in the back of a gleaming black Range Rover. It was the Evoque model. She knew this as it was one of her choices when she finally decided to trade in her BMW X5. Nina thought it funny, that being shoved into the back of a car, with a Glock tucked under her ribs, swiftly put her off the model.

Barney, on the other hand, was dragged off the aircraft. His hands were still bound but now he had three layers of gaffer tape fixed to his mouth. It was in everyone's best interests to keep him silent rather than Taser him again.

The two British henchmen that Rogue had brought to the agency office were standing next to the Range Rover, but they let the misplaced Spanish policemen put the big man into the back of the vehicle.

"Are you ok?" Nina asked but immediately made her idiot face, glancing at the tape across Barney's mouth.

Barney returned with his idiot face, nodded he was ok and gestured with his head toward Rogue.

The malevolent Mindsweeper stood at the mouth of the hangar, a mobile phone pinned to his ear. Whatever the conversation, it was brief. The phone was dropped into a suit jacket pocket and Rogue made his way to the car.

He peered into the vehicle, eyeing his captives, sensing their value but only as a means to an end. They were the bait for Rogue's trap.

"Mr Dean is on his way. Soon you'll all be reunited." There was no optimism in the tone of the statement.

He didn't wait for a reply. Rogue turned and walked back toward the gaping yawn of the hangar door.

In the distance, he could hear a vehicle approaching on the service road. This could only be the Audi of Raymond Dean.

While he stood with eager anticipation of his own reunion with Roxana, Rogue could feel something. Somewhere in the depths of his own mind was a sensation that he had not felt since he was a teenager. It was the sensation he had felt while learning to merge his mind with the other psychics in the group. But this was new. This was different.

There was another with the ability; nearby. It was not Ghost as his presence was too familiar. But also it was not Spook and it definitely wasn't his Angel Roxana. It was not a familiar signature at all.

Whoever it was, they were powerful. And they were close.

# Chapter Fifty One

The beaten up old blue Vauxhall Astra was parked in the make shift layby, on the service road running parallel to the runway. Pete rested against the bonnet, can of Red Bull in hand, after bidding farewell and good luck to his employer.

Pete had been sent to babysit the psychics whilst Ray planned to play a gambit to rescue Nina and Barney. He didn't know the plan but he knew that his boss would be winging it, and it wouldn't be pretty.

Sitting in the back of the car, were Roxana and Spook. They munched on sandwiches and crisps, and drank bottled water provided by their new chaperone.

Roxana wanted to read Pete's mind but thought it too dangerous to do so in close proximity to Rogue and Ghost.

They may have been parked in a secluded spot, hidden from a direct line of sight from their pursuers, but it hadn't escaped her or Spook's attention that the tail of the SAED company jet was partially protruding from the far hangar, almost a mile away.

Pete approached the rear of the car and leaned into the open door. He was curious about his passengers.

"So you guys are real live Mindsweepers?" He weighted the query as though he were asking if they were musicians.

"We are." she wanted so badly to enter the man's head to see if it was a sceptical or serious question.

"It's ok, I've read up loads of stuff and I'm cool with all the kinda things you guys have had to do."

Roxana sat up, changing her stance. Her brow furrowed, pre-warning the young man that she was not amused by his statement and that a rebuke would be forthcoming.

"While you might be *'cool'* with all the stuff we've done. We are far from 'cool' with it. We have intruded into innocent minds, taken their ideas, stole their dreams, and much, much worse. If you put yourself into someone's mind then you have to be fully prepared to absorb a part of their soul. You feel their feelings. You feel their pain. You experience the very darkest thoughts of the most damaged individuals you could ever wish to meet. Trust me when I say, we are not superheroes of any kind. I have merged my mind with so many brutalised women that I have felt their violation, suffered their shame and cried an ocean after living through their experiences. Being one of us is not like playing a first person computer game. You can't just hit the 'off' button when you're done; roll over and go to sleep. The echoes of another human being's consciousness can stay with you for days, weeks, and even months," Tears flowed, Roxana's initial rage was now the bitter sorrow that sucked any of the joy from her life, "Some of the bleakest thoughts never leave you. They are like scars. They may fade but they never, ever disappear. You can't cover them up. You can't cut them out. They are always there, always visible and always reminding you of the immoral things that you have perpetrated on too many…"

Her shoulders shuddered as the burden of her existence overwhelmed her, cutting the flow of rambling words.

Spook offered a shoulder as comfort, hugging the petite psychic into his lanky frame. He knew her burden; he, more than any other, had experienced the torment of their shared ability. He was damaged beyond repair. His mind was fragmented. He knew that unless there was some kind of respite, his mind would unfold and collapse.

Pete stood in shamed silence, wishing he had said nothing. He stood by as the pair comforted each other. Companions that lived in a different world to most; an evil, twisted world where there were no secrets, no surprises, nothing hidden; until now.

Instantaneously, the psychics reacted. Something was wrong. Roxana looked at Spook. Spook stared back into her bottomless black eyes.

They could sense it.

There was another psychic; another Mindsweeper.

Try as they might, they could not block the intrusion.

This amount of power was way beyond anything they had experienced before. This was not Rogue, or Ghost. This was something very different and they were vulnerable. They were weak.

# Chapter Fifty Two

The twilight blackened the clouds against the burning orange sky, whilst making the bright white hangars appear an opaque blue against the skyline. As the sun dropped from view, the heat in the air rapidly dissipated, cooling everything but the rage Ray felt flowing through his veins. With a flurry of loose chippings and dry soil, the Audi powered onto the runway. He only gave a cursory, sideways glance, to see if there was an aircraft about to land right on top of him. There wasn't.

He spied Rogue standing just outside of the hangar door. Waiting for the prize he hoped Ray was about to deliver no doubt.

The thought of running down the crazed psychic had flitted across his mind but was soon dismissed. He couldn't predict what contingency plan had been put in place by Rogue. So Ray would play it safe.

As he neared the solitary figure Ray could see the puzzled look blazing across Rogue's face. He wondered if only one body in the car was the issue. But when he halted the car right next to the suit cladded man; Rogue wasn't even looking at the car.

Ray stepped out of the vehicle but left the engine running.

"Where are Nina and Barney?" he dispensed with the pleasantries.

"Where are my Mindsweepers?" Rogue focused on the investigator now.

"You'll get them when my people are safely away from here,"

"Then we have a dilemma, don't we." Rogue's eyes drifted off into the distance, as if searching for his 'Mindsweepers' or something else maybe.

"I think we do." Ray said, looking over his own shoulder trying to see what had captured Rogue's attention.

"Tell me, Mr Dean, have you come across any others like us?"

"I don't understand."

Before the Psychic could reply there was a disturbance back in the hangar. Ray noticed a young olive skinned man dashing toward them. He assumed this was Ghost. He assumed correctly.

"What is it Jakub?" Rogue turned to receive whatever his minion psychic was about to say but there was a harshness to his tone.

"Can you sense them?" the words were spat out with a heavy Polish accent.

"If Roxana does not want to be..." Rogue was cut off.

"Not Roxana! The other Mindsweeper!" Ghost was clearly panicked.

"Shut it, Jakub. Don't lose your head. Just bring out our guests for Mr Dean to see." Although the usual arrogance delivered the statement, there was a nervy tremor in Rogue's voice.

Ray could feel that all was not well in the opposition camp.

The head psychic watched his anxious colleague head back toward the black Range Rover before reengaging with the investigator.

"Sorry for that interruption Mr Dean, as I was saying. Have you come across any other Mindsweepers?"

It was obvious now that there was something disturbing the usually calm and collected Rogue.

What it was, Ray didn't have a clue, but he was known for thinking on his feet and hoped that he could outsmart the ruthless bastard who stood before him now.

"I've met many people during my investigations, Hogarth, or is it Sanchez?" Ray smirked as he uttered the name, "Whatever you wish to call yourself, I have met some crazy, yet brilliant individuals along the way and this case is no different. I have also met some deranged, psychotic nut jobs in my time and you really do take the gold medal from that pile."

"TELL ME MR DEAN!" the blood engorged Rogue's Latin American cheeks as he screamed his demands, "WHO ARE YOU USING?"

The bait was taken. Ray just needed to land the biggest fish he had ever encountered. He prayed his gambit would work.

"The Russians run programmes using psychics too don't they?" Ray smiled a confident smile and even forced a laugh as he saw the wide eyed gaze of Miguel 'Rogue' Sanchez, a fearless psychic, now with something to fear.

Rogue reached into his jacket and stepped toward the investigator.

"I might not be able to get into your brain but that won't stop me putting a bullet through it." Rogue levelled an automatic pistol at Ray's face.

"I don't believe you would come this far just to shoot me and then go home empty handed." Ray could smell the mix of cordite and gun oil from the muzzle as it hovered just an inch or two from his face.

"I'm going to shoot you anyway, but if you don't tell me who you are using, or where Roxana is, I'm going to shoot your friends first." A calmer psychotic tone returned to Rogue's voice.

"You'll get what you want when they are safe, and not before." Ray's poker face cracked at the sight of Nina being frogmarched toward him by Ghost. Barney was slightly behind them, flanked by the two thugs that had accompanied Rogue to the office.

Rogue broke eye contact as soon as he had seen a flicker of hesitancy flash across Ray's face, as the investigator's eyes were drawn toward his approaching friends; more so toward Nina.

"Ah, here they are! Which one shall I shoot first Mr Dean?"

"The Polish one maybe." Ray's quipped.

Barney laughed through his gaffer taped lips only to be punched in the side by the larger, younger thug.

"Very funny, Mr Dean," Rogue wasn't showing any amusement, "how funny would it be if Mr Barnett had a bullet hole in him?"

He stayed silent. Ray could see that the game was drawing to a close and he wasn't playing with his best pieces. The time for thinking was over. Action was the only option now but anything less than miraculous perfection might result in a casualty, or worse; a corpse.

"No more jokes, Mr Dean?" the psychic provoked, "If we are done with all this frivolity then I'd like to know where my people are."

"Why are you not using your psychic powers?" It was serious question.

"You know why, Mr Dean,"

"I'm afraid I don't Mr Sanchez. As I told you before, I'm not a psychic whisperer or anything like that. I'm just a guy that got involved in a case that I shouldn't have."

"Then who, and where, is the other Mindsweeper?" Rogue posed the question, but there was doubt whether a suitable answer would be forthcoming.

Ray wanted to delay his answer, and delay the inevitable, but there were no more moves to play other than a plea for mercy to buy some time.

"I don't know of any other Mindsweeper or any other psychics. Please let them go," Ray raised his open hands in a gesture that he had nothing left to give but himself, "let them go, and keep me, and I will have your Mindsweepers delivered to you."

Rogue turned on the spot, placing the muzzle of his gun next to Nina's head.

"Make the call and bring my people here, now, or I'll shoot them both and keep you anyway."

A sickening sensation hit Ray square in the gut. He thought he may vomit as burning bile rose in his throat. The sight of a gun, pressed against the head of the woman he loved was more than enough, but to actually see the fear in her eyes as it happened made him realise he wasn't in the position to keep up this bluff. And it was a bluff.

"OK, OK."

Ray reached into his pocket for his phone. He punched in the number. When the phone was answered, the instruction was given.

Within half a minute of the phone being placed back into Ray's pocket, a car could be heard travelling along the service road. What was going to happen next was anybody's guess. But the bad guys had guns. And Ray, well he had nothing.

# Chapter Fifty Three

The dusty blue Astra pulled up next to Ray's immaculate black Audi A3. Dented and worthless it may have looked, but the passengers made the vehicle far more valuable than the German made car beside it.

Pete stayed at the wheel, engine running, as both Roxana and Spook stepped out.

It was the moment of truth for the Mindsweepers. Not just the two runaways, but for all of them.

Rogue turned his focus toward his rebellious colleagues but took aim at Ray once more.

"Ah, Roxana, you look radiant," Rogue's words were drenched in his sarcasm, "and Jamie, you look…homeless,"

"And you look like a power crazed psychopath, Miguel," Roxana was chancing her answer.

Spook stayed silent.

"Just top dog as usual," his bravado was not convincing.

"You're not top dog, you never were. You always lurked in the shadows of others better than you. You may have blinded Shriver with your scheming but he's no longer here." Roxana was relentless, "The financing of your personal crusade is over. The Mindsweepers are over."

Rogue licked his lips nervously. The firearm twitched in his grip, her words had stung his soul.

"You may have made Shriver take that dive but you haven't stopped anything, Roxana." The smug smile looked ill-placed on his sweaty, trembling face.

"What are you talking about, Miguel?" she took a few steps away from the car, toward her antagonist but maintaining a safe distance, "There is no more money. No more program. No more research. What are you and Jakub going to do? Become freelancers?"

"Oh Roxy," he knew that she hated that abbreviated form of her name, "I am the sole benefactor of Shriver's will."

There was no need for words. Her stunned silence was enough of a response.

"And I didn't even have to kill him or make it look like an accident," Rogue's insipid glee oozed, "I let you do that. I let you believe that he wanted to harvest an army of Mindsweepers. I let you believe he was pulling all the strings. I've been controlling

Shriver for as long as I can remember. Since I first made him buy me ice cream as a child. I manipulated his lawyers and his advisors to make decisions that couldn't be undone after his death. I've controlled everything about SAED for the last twenty five years or so."

"But how, you were a child?" she asked incredulously.

"You know the transfer of knowledge is a two way street with us, we learn from the subject and we make the decisions for them. Make enough decisions, over a long period of time, and suddenly the subject will start to think like the controlling Mindsweeper. I just kept pushing him to make more and more money, until I became old enough to realise that shrewd business deals on a global market will not only make more money but will also have other businesses running toward you, throwing money and shares in your direction. I built that company up with the naïve greed of a child. Why do you think I always got my way?"

"I handed it all to you on a plate?" The words nearly choked her.

"That's right. I now hold the controlling percentage of SAED. And Ghost took out the owner of Roux L'aeronautique, Vincent Roux, so that his grieving wife will be obliged to sell on that company and ALL of its patents. That will make me Chief Executive Officer for the largest defence company on the planet." Rogue's eyes shined an omnipotent gleam, "It's not over Roxana. It's only just begun. There will always be Mindsweepers. And the next generation is growing, right there, in your belly."

Rage, fear and hatred collided; the big bang deep within the soul of the mother to be. The protective instinct would be unfathomable from such a unique woman with an uncompromising ability.

"NEVER!!!" Roxana screamed at her tormentor.

Almost instantly, the Mindsweepers seemed to come alive. The overwhelming power of the fifth Mindsweeper dissolved, releasing the four deadly psychics, returning their abilities.

Ray noticed the changes and reacted instantly. He stepped aside from the path of the bullet that was idling within the chamber pointing at his chest and lunged toward the psychic, closing the distance between them.

Rogue was distracted momentarily from the return of his ability and didn't see the elbow driving into the centre of his face, until the blinding flash of pain awoke and stunned all senses simultaneously.

Ray gripped the firearm and twisted it free from his aggressor's hand. He hadn't expected the move to work so easily.

It was a moment for time to stand still. Nobody moved. Nobody breathed. Nobody knew their next move.

But, from the back of the hangar, the echo of a car door slamming launched urgency back into the equation.

"RUN!" Ray yelled at his colleagues as he levelled the weapon at Rogue.

Barney took advantage of the situation. He raised his arms and swung them down swiftly, his elbows passing outside his body, whilst the cable tie that bound his wrists was forced to breaking point against his taut waistline and the pivoting of his arms. There was even enough inertia in the movement to carry a trailing elbow into the solar plexus of the older, caveman-like henchman to his left, dropping him to the ground. Barney span on his toes, driving a fist into the throat of the larger, younger henchman. The man went down easy.

Nina sprinted to the Audi, jumping into the driver's seat. The keys were in the ignition. The engine was running and revving almost immediately.

"COME ON!!" she screamed.

Barney was now trading blows with the older henchman, who had recovered faster than he would have liked.

Ray stood surprisingly calm, the pistol still in his hand and aiming centre mass. He caught sight of the two Spanish police officers running toward the commotion, guns in hand.

"Barney, get out of here," Ray voice didn't falter under the incredible pressure he should have felt. He had gotten to his lover and his friend in an attempt to save them. Now was not the time to let his resolve crack again. It was so different when he was consumed by the helplessness that the kidnapping had created in him. He never wanted to feel that way again.

Barney did as he was told but not without crashing his fist into the nose bone of the caveman and kneeing the recovering younger man in the face.

"Let it go Sanchez," Ray uttered, "let them all go. You're not good enough to stop a bullet."

Before a reply could form from Rogue's lips, a barrage of gunshots rang out. The Spanish cops were shooting.

Ray took his eyes off the psychic for a moment. Everything seemed to be happening too fast, yet he was reacting in slow motion.

He watched Barney fall, face down on to the tarmac; a patch of red growing, seeping through his khaki T-shirt.

There were also three bullet holes in the Audi; one in the driver side door, two in the driver side window. Behind the shattered glass there was no silhouette of Nina as there should have been.

Ray pointed the pistol over Rogue's shoulder, toward the Spanish gunmen, and fired, and fired, and fired until the clip was empty. No more bullets - no more options.

# Chapter Fifty Four

The gun shots awoke Roxana from her trance. She too had been released from the grip of the fifth Mindsweeper but instead of taking the chance to use her regained ability to assist in the fight, she had immediately tried searching for the unknown psychic.

Her mind had taken her somewhere but she was baffled by the destination. Once she had linked to any subject, Roxana would be able see with their eyes, hear with their ears and touch with their fingers, but there was none of this. She could see nothing but blackness; hear nothing, not even a heartbeat during a held breath; and there was no sensation of touch at all. Her ability had taken her to the place she wanted to go, but where it was, just wasn't right.

She wanted to go deeper but somehow the might of her ability was compromised, or so it seemed.

Roxana linked with Spook, taking him into the trance. Maybe together they could find out who the individual was. Whoever it was, they were formidable, with such power that it rendered the other Mindsweepers useless.

Long thought to be the pinnacle of their kind, Roxana and Spook felt utterly mortal, just as the many innocents whose lives they had ruined or intruded on.

No matter the depth of the intrusion, there was no conscious mind to dwell in or memories to read. To them it was similar to switching on the TV and having no reception, not even white noise. But none of that mattered now.

It had been the shots fired by the Spanish policemen that had pulled her back into reality. In her stunned state she observed Ray return fire. It was clear that he had never fired a pistol before. She watched the firearm recoil in his hand. None of his bullets found a target. His inexperience was obvious, and as the chamber clicked empty, his plight too.

As the corrupt cops refocused their aim on the investigator, Roxana refocused herself. Even with the psychic barriers placed into the minds of the Spanish men, she entered both easily.

To all those looking on, the men stopped dead in their tracks. Gun hands fell to their sides, momentarily, before being raised one final time. The firearm's muzzles were pushed against the rooves of their mouths. The movement was flawlessly synchronised, almost robotic. Even the trigger pulls and resulting gunshots were executed simultaneously. The two Spanish cops dropped where they had stood, as the backs of their skulls exploded in a mess of bone and brain matter.

"ROXANA!!" Rogue's scream echoed within the dull steel shell of the hangar.

"It ends here Miguel," she answered calmly, "it ends now."

"It ends when I say it ends. I have the funds, I have the means. And I now have the future growing in your womb."

"MY child will NEVER be your puppet."

"Our child, ANGEL, our child."

"I am not YOUR Angel. I will never be YOUR Angel." Her voice lifted in rage. She had never wanted to be a part of the programme. And never would be a part of the programme again. For Roxana to live; for her child to live; there had to be no more Angel.

"Things could have been so different. If only you could have seen that." Rogue's manner returned to that of a calm psychotic once more.

"They will be different - different for me and my child."

"That child is half my genes. You cannot predict how he or she will be, can you?"

She knew he spoke the truth. Throughout their lives they had encountered too many with abilities like their own who could not handle the responsibility of the power. The merging of minds, from the very timid to the very strongest of wills, changed the psychic, and not for the better. Traits, fears, and experiences swirled within the cerebral soup and were added to the memories of those who could walk through a person's mind just as though they were walking through a meadow. The ease of their power made it as natural as any other sense they possessed. The manipulation of that skill was made even easier by the very specific training they had spent their entire youth mastering. Roxana knew that her child would be no different. The sixth sense of a pure bred pedigree, super psychic would have no limits and try as she might to raise the child to be different, she could not predict the ability her unborn. Unlike her, there may be no way to switch off the psychic ability, like there was no way to switch off the sense of vision or hearing. She was able to do it but she was unique, as they all were. They were all products of their environment, and individual abilities created individual environments. Once born, no one could predict how much that empty vessel would absorb, which traits would dominate. But Rogue was unlikely to let one of his own, with such a power, just slip away; and especially not when genetically, the child would be half Rogue. Roxana had to end it, now. But how was the question she didn't want to answer herself.

# Chapter Fifty Five

He had watched the men place the guns in their mouths. He had watched their bodies fall to the ground. And now he watched the exchange between Rogue and Roxana. Ray was literally fused in place, not wanting to move toward his stricken friend or to look into the car pocked with bullet holes. Too afraid of what he would see.

He never viewed Nina as anything less than perfect. She had changed his life, for the better, in so many ways. What awaited him inside that car may bring relief or the cruel devastation of his worst fears.

Ray snapped out of his stationary condition. He pushed himself away from Rogue and toward the figure on the ground.

As he placed a hand on Barney's shoulder, he was relieved to see his friend react to the contact.

Barney rolled over, pain etched into his face. The bullet had entered his left shoulder blade and exited just below his left collar bone.

A concerned smile was all Ray could muster for his friend before his attention was drawn to movement from within the Audi.

The apprehension was short lived as he approached the vehicle to see Nina's wide blue eyes blink, as she rose from the foetal position she had assumed across the front seats of the car.

He pulled the door open and could immediately see where one bullet had harmlessly entered the seat and the other had hit the steering wheel and been deflected by the steel core of the steering column. Regardless of the impact on the vehicle, none of the rounds had hit Nina. She was shaken, but unharmed.

He pulled her from the car. His arms encircled her taut, yet trembling form. To him, an eternity had passed since they had last embraced. And although he never wanted to release her again, he knew that time was of the essence and they had to move, with urgency.

Turning his attention back to Barney, Ray lifted his stricken friend to his feet and eased him in to the back of the car.

Nina got in beside their injured comrade. She took off her thin cotton jacket and immediately applied pressure to the wound with it.

Almost forgotten in the frenzy of gunplay, Ray noticed Pete crouching behind the Astra. The young man's eyes were saucer wide and darting to and fro, as he waited to see what happened next.

"Pete," Ray yelled to his frightened colleague, "Barney's been hurt."

Immediately, the young man responded, running toward the Audi.

"What can I do?"

"Take my car and get him to hospital." Ray almost pushed Pete into the driving seat.

Pete took his place behind the wheel and handed his Astra keys to Ray without being asked.

"What are you gonna do?" Nina posed the question.

"Whatever it takes to keep you safe." Ray replied.

"A bulletproof vest would be nice." Barney winced out a joke.

"Too late for that now." Ray said.

"Nine years in the Army, ten years with the Police force, and I take a bullet working with you." the big man smiled through gritted teeth.

Ray merely returned the smile, no comment would be appropriate.

He slammed the driver's door and hammered a fist onto the roof.

The instruction was obviously understood as the Audi's wheels bit into the Tarmac, pulling away at speed toward the service road.

Ray hoped that now his colleagues, and lover, might be safe from harm. It would have been so easy to get into the car and escape with them, but as he knew only too well, the Mindsweepers can get you anywhere. He had to see this to the bitter end.

# Chapter Fifty Six

They watched the Audi disappear in a powdery cloud of dust and grit from the service road, as it made haste toward a possible sanctuary. Roxana turned her gaze to Ray and wondered why he had chosen to stay. She didn't need him there. She didn't need his help anymore. Things were starting to fall into place now.

"You don't think they're safe do you Mr Dean?" Rogue stood tall, but somehow seemed less important. The air of defiance was still present in his voice yet it came across as bravado, as though he didn't believe the words he was speaking.

Ray remained silent.

"Do you think that you can harm them, Miguel?" Roxana replied to the question, "You've lost your nerve, haven't you?"

"I've lost nothing." If there was to be a further comment, it was cut short.

"I can feel that the confidence has left you. We all can."

Rogue glanced in all directions; first at Ghost, then at Spook and finally back to Roxana. He didn't even look at his remaining henchmen, who had now fully recovered from their exchange with Barney and stood idly, waiting for instruction but not brandishing any weapons.

"I may not be as gifted as you, Roxana, but my ability has always been superior to these two." With more bravado and gesturing he tried to bluff his way out of the corner but he knew that talk was cheap. Actions spoke louder than words, so they say. His action would have to extinguish their insurrection.

"It's no longer about superiority, Miguel. It's about moving past what we were, and moving toward what we will be." Roxana controlled her words but her eyes darted toward Spook, who had remained silent the entire time.

Spook nodded his head in agreement. He was done with it all too.

"You can't just walk away from all that we've achieved. We are linked forever." Rogue mirrored her action and looked toward Ghost, who nodded his head just once.

"Links can be broken. Jamie and I will take ourselves away. Live in isolation if we have to but we will not be part of this anymore. There will be no Spook and there will be no Angel." She remained firm.

"What about this new, unseen, Mindsweeper? You felt it too. There is another out there who is more powerful than you." The maniacal confidence slowly crept back onto Rogue's breath as he uttered the statement.

"I know Miguel, but they will never hurt me."

"You were never one to bluff Roxana. You don't even know who it is. I could feel your confusion when we were all linked."

She stood silently for a moment, pondering on which way to deliver the news. Wondering how it would be received. Rogue had closed his mind to her, intrusion was of no assistance now, she would have to say it and hope for the best. But also be prepared for the worse.

"I know who the other Mindsweeper is and they will never hurt me, or any one, I wouldn't allow it."

"I think you overestimate your…" Rogue's sentence was cut when he saw Roxana's hands nurturing the small swelling in her abdomen. Of course, it was obvious now. Who could be more powerful than the four most powerful psychics ever to breathe air? The answer was the unborn bastard spawn of two of those psychics; unborn and yet to breathe air but already so formidable as to render all others powerless with a single thought; the very first thought.

Within the muted echo of the hangar, rage screamed without sound from Rogue.

Roxana cast a glance across all faces. Rogue raged, while Ghost appeared confused. The henchmen stood silently, not daring to move. It had not been lost on them that their Spanish counterparts had been taken out of the equation swiftly, so they kept weapons holstered and the threat level low.

Ray was like a spare piece of the puzzle, he had been brought in as the subject of revenge but now his role in this charade seemed pointless. Roxana felt nothing but gratitude for the investigator, in a direct contradiction of Rogue's feelings.

Could they just walk away? Unlikely.

Somewhere from outside the hangar was a noise; a low droning noise.

Eyes darted back and forth.

Only Rogue's didn't move. His pupils were fixed onto his antagonist, burning into her, with hatred and distain.

The droning grew closer.

Roxana returned the stare but could see that as focused as Rogue's gaze was, his full attention was not on her. He was linked to someone.

The droning noise was very obvious to everyone now.

A vehicle was approaching, rapidly.

A panic seemed to spark, as the majority of the souls could not predict what would happen next.

There was a screech of tyre squeal as a refuelling truck loomed from nowhere, arcing toward the hangar opening.

Ray rolled out of the way, but he was not the target.

Roxana was transfixed as the front grill bore down on her. Unseen hands grabbed her, wrenching the mother-to-be out from the path of what would have been certain death. When she looked up Spook was standing over her, the unseen hands were his.

All eyes watched as the truck careered on two wheels into the rear of the parked aircraft, smashing one of the jet engines that straddled the tail. There was an instant stench of kerosene as fuel lines were severed and flammable liquid gushed onto the hangar floor. The Refuelling truck fell onto its side and more fuel began to pour from damaged vehicle.

Fury overwhelmed Rogue. He reached into the jacket of the nearest henchman and pulled a firearm from a holster. The first shot was nowhere close, giving Roxana time to react. A second shot was fired, this time it hit a target, but not *the* target. Not Roxana.

Spook hit the ground hard as the round clipped him in the side. His body contorted with the burning blow just below the ribs.

Roxana immediately went to his aid, trying to drag the gangly giant back to his feet and out of harm's way.

"SANCHEZ!" Ray bellowed a distraction but it only brought the aim of the gun in his direction.

Rogue fired again but his skill was also not with a firearm.

Ray evaded one shot, sprinting for the cover of the Astra before a second was fired. He peered over the door frame with the hope that his outburst had bought Roxana and Spook enough time to get to cover.

Roxana had bundled Spook into the Range Rover and was about to jump into the driver's seat when a bullet pierced the rear windscreen. She ducked down into the foot well for cover, as another round hit the one of the side windows, cubes of glass scattering in all directions. Panicked, she reached for the glove compartment to look for keys; there were none. But there was a handgun.

Another bullet hit the car, piercing the roof.

The weapon felt heavy and cumbersome in her delicate hand but she knew this was the only way for her now. A quick glance through the gap in the headrest showed her aggressor advancing, flanked by his goons. Rogue had the pistol pointed toward the car. Ghost stood next to him, unarmed. The henchmen brought up the rear, looking perplexed by the unfolding events before him.

Roxana flicked off the safety catch, took aim and fired into the group. The bullet ricocheted off the hangar floor, the group scattered. She fired again, and again, and again. Not really aiming or looking to see where the bullets hit, she continued to pull on the trigger hoping to hit something.

She did.

A misplaced round pinged off the chassis of the overturned truck and showered sparks into the sea of aviation fuel that had continued to spread across the hangar floor.

The floor went up. There was an audible whoosh. Liquid became fire. Air became superheated.

The flash sent Ray, who was just outside the hangar, diving for cover. The heat seared the oxygen out of the air. He squeezed his lids shut against the temperature that seemed to boil his eyes in their sockets. His instinct was to crawl away from the heat source; eyes shut or not. When he reached what felt like a safe distance he turned back toward the now, burning building. He could just make out the Range Rover deep inside the hangar and what looked to be the figure of a man still holding a gun.

\*

The henchmen were gone. Ghost was gone. Deep within the steel sheet and girder building, Rogue still held the pistol and walked right up to the Range Rover. Roxana's magazine had spent its last round. There was no longer a need for him to cower away from returned gunfire.

Rogue took aim between the beautiful black eyes that peered from the driver's seat. There was no escape from their fate now. This had to be the end of them; for their kind. But if it was to end, it would be under Rogue's terms. They were his. He would say if they lived or died. And he would rather them all dead than to live a life without his command.

He pulled the trigger. The gun clicked empty. He pulled again. Again it clicked.

Rogue hurled the pistol at the window shattering the glass, removing the last barrier between him and the Mindsweeper he had wanted to be. The most powerful, the most respected, the most loved. He looked into those eyes and knew he was defeated.

All of a sudden, the rear door burst open, the wounded Spook launched himself toward their maniacal leader. His massive hands gripped Rogue's throat, crushing down on the smaller man. Years of hatred and torture fuelled the rage. Never before had the young psychic been able to lay his hands upon his tormenter, without swift reprisal.

The fight would be short lived.

The flames that engulfed the refuelling truck, had found a way into the compact steel skin to seek out more of the much needed liquid to continue the burn. The aviation fuel, tightly packed into the steel tube, rapidly expanded as it ignited into a fireball. It consumed the aircraft, lifting the roof from the building, as the shockwave forced everything outward, with scorching ferocity and scattering burning debris in all directions. The Carnage of the inferno was impossible to survive. The hangar and all of its contents were afire.

*

His singed eyes opened. Maybe he had expected to be opening them on some version of heaven but instead he witnessed a vision of a living hell. The blast had thrown his body clear, dumping Ray almost into the bushes. There were puddles of fire and twisted pieces of scorched metal littering the rough tarmac within his view.

With an effort, Ray stood up and looked back toward the hangar. What stood in its place was a charred, burning wound in the ground. The walls had been punched outward, whilst the roof had been blasted skyward, only to fall back, in pieces, onto the wreckage within. Nothing could have survived.

He looked at the broken form of Pete's Astra. A wheel from the truck had been propelled through the driver's door and had exited out of the roof, opening the vehicle like a sardine can.

He dropped the keys into his pocket and walked away.


The early evening was illuminated by the flames. Trudging the length of the gritty concrete service road, his shadow flickered with the ever changing flames that lit his way. The air was uncomfortably warm and filled with the sound of distant sirens of the approaching emergency vehicles. Ray hoped to avoid the police until he had discovered what had happened to Nina, Barney and Pete.

From within the confines of a pocket, his phone rang. He dug deep, pulling it from his jacket and swiped the cracked screen to answer the call. It had come from Pete's phone but the voice was Nina.

They had made it to a hospital. Barney was in emergency surgery but not thought to be in critical condition. Nina was shaken up, as was Pete. But they were alive and that was all that mattered to Ray.

The case that he deemed too dangerous to take, but was forced into, had been survived. But only just. Physical scars heal. Mental ones linger on. He prayed that he would never hear the term Mindsweeper or talk of psychics again.

But deep down, he knew that would not be the case. He knew that all his efforts would be measured against such extraordinary individuals in the future.

But who knew what the future would now hold, Ray certainly didn't.

# Chapter Fifty Seven

Five Years Later

The Mediterranean sun beat down on the spotlessly clean streets. Heat trapped in the tarmac and concrete paths could be felt through the soles of shoes, even when shade had fallen over the hardened floor, the surface of the Spanish streets still radiated warmth.

They walked along the marina, taking in the view of wealth moored at every berth. Yachts and cruisers of all different shapes and sizes, created a landscape all of their own. Brilliant white vessels glowing whiter in the midday brightness, almost to the point of blinding those that dared to stare too long at millions of Euros of floating excess. The playground of the rich and famous lived up to its name; expensive boats, expensive cars, and folk with expensive tastes. The opulence was everywhere.

A large concrete barrier made an ideal seat for them to sit and watch the vibrant life of Puerto Banus, the streets were its veins, the people its blood. As long as the people flowed, the town was alive, and this town was alive twenty four hours a day.

Even whilst seated their hands stayed locked together, as though the break in that physical contact would divide them emotionally, but in reality, that would never happen.

She looked at him and smiled. He returned the gaze and the smile. They had seen these streets so many times before but not like this. Not with their own eyes, always with someone else's.

He asked a question, but not one that could be heard.

"Always say it out loud." his mother said.

"Is this where your dreams take you?" It was a mature question for a four year old, but then he was no ordinary four year old.

"Sometimes," she smiled, "my dreams take me lots of places. But then you know that."

The child did not reply. He knew her dreams as well as he knew his own. They were linked at the heart like only a mother and child can be. But they were also linked at the mind like no others that had come before.

Little Jamie, named after his mother's only true friend, often watched her dreams and nightmares from the inside, and intervened where he could to lessen the darkness that inhabited her sleep. Sometimes he could ease her painful slumber, sometimes he couldn't. He could never help during the 'Fire Dream'.

He never asked about it but he knew all the details, like he knew everything else. He saw the flames that trapped her in the car. He felt the explosion within the tight confines of the metal building. He saw the car forced through the buckling steel wall by the blast. He felt the flames burn her skin as she managed to escape the burning vehicle. He felt it all.

The scars that covered her face, head and arms had healed before he was born. But still he felt them. He felt all things in all people. The power he wielded was far beyond anything possessed by anyone that had come before him. How he would use that power was only something that time would tell, but for now, he would keep it hidden, in the same way his mother would keep him hidden.

The only way to predict the future is to create it, and his future would be as a Mindsweeper like no other.

Printed in Great Britain
by Amazon